Thomas Cooper De Leon

**The Puritan's Daughter**

Thomas Cooper De Leon

**The Puritan's Daughter**

ISBN/EAN: 9783337351052

Printed in Europe, USA, Canada, Australia, Japan

Cover: Foto ©Andreas Hilbeck / pixelio.de

More available books at **www.hansebooks.com**

# THE

# PURITAN'S DAUGHTER:

[ SEQUEL TO " CREOLE AND PURITAN."]

## A CHARACTER ROMANCE OF TWO SECTIONS.

## BY T. C. DE LEON,

Author of " FOUR YEARS IN REBEL CAPITALS," "JUNY, OR ONLY
ONE GIRL'S STORY," "SYBILLA, A ROMAUNT OF
THE TOWN," ETC., ETC.

---

" I am all the daughters of my father's house,
  And all the brothers, too."            [ *Twelfth Night.*

" And thus the soldier, armed with resolution,
  Told his soft tale and was thriving wooer "
                                    [ *Colley Cibber.*

MOBILE, ALA.:
THE GOSSIP PRINTING COMPANY.
1891.

TO

# Colonel Alex. K. McClure,

### OF PHILADELPHIA,

IN TOKEN OF RESPECT FOR ONE WHO HAS PROVED

TRUE TO BOTH SECTIONS OF A COMMON

COUNTRY BY REMAINING TRUE

TO HIMSELF,

THIS ROMANCE OF REALITY IS INSCRIBED.

—— By the Same Author.—New Edition.—376 Large Pages—Cloth ——
Prepaid on Receipt of $1.25.

# Four Years in Rebel Capitals.

## AN INSIDE VIEW OF SOCIAL LIFE IN THE SOUTHERN CONFEDERACY FROM BIRTH TO DEATH.

### FROM ORIGINAL NOTES MADE FROM 1861 TO 1865

### BY T. C. DE LEON.

"It is valuable to the student and particularly interesting to the general reader."—*Boston Globe.*

"Should be in every library and every bookcase, for frequent perusal and constant reference."—*Augusta News.*

"Is more valuable, as it is far more readable, than any history of the Southern cause that has yet been written.'"—*San Francisco Chronicle.*

"The Grand Old Man" says, in a recent letter to the author: "I write to thank you for your volume, 'Four Years in Rebel Capitals,' which I have read with very lively interest. Faithfully yours,

"Wm. E. Gladstone."

Mrs. Augusta Evans Wilson, the famous authoress, writes. "Accept my cordial congratulations upon the polished and elegant diction, the genuine pathos, the unanswerable logic and the brilliant, critical acumen that characterize your last and—may I add? incomparably best book."

Jas. R. Randall, the poet critic, writes in the "Catholic Mirror:" "It has not a dull page, but many bright, witty, pathetic and dramatic chapters. * * * In some respects this work is the prose epic of the bloody Confederate drama."

"Mr. De Leon has written a book which possesses a distinctive character. Although giving us stirring accounts of the fighting, he has written a book which is a great deal more than a mere military history."—*London Times.*

"Mr. De Leon does not offer the stale husks, but gives us the most full and picturesque account of the great struggle of any we have ever read."—*London Telegraph.*

# PUBLISHER'S PREFACE.

The success of Mr. De Leon's novel, "Creole and Puritan,"
—first published in Lippincott's Magazine—was truly excep-
tional; equally from its wide sale and from the comment it
drew from the press and from careful thinkers, North and
South.

In many instances discussion of the motive and lesson of
the story was carried from the critical departments of leading
journals into their editorial columns. The broad catholic
spirit—"Which yields no tittle of principle, but breathes progressive advance among the thinkers of the South," as one
writer said—was accepted as true reflex of what cant mis-
names "The New South;" but what is, in reality, the old South
of yesterday, girding her loins afresh and donning the fair pan-
oply of common sense, to do her *devoir* in the busy battle of
to-day.

The Hon. Henry Watterson said, in course of a long leading editorial on this book in the *Courier-Journal* ·

"It offers not a little to arrest the attention of thinking people, at
the same time that, in literary and artistic qualities, it strikes far above
the current standard.

"As a psychologic study, it abounds in keen flashes of penetrating
and enlightened observation, permeated throughout by two elements
most unusual to such productions—a simple, touching pathos on the
side of character; and also such public aspects and belongings as are
incident to a stream of reflection, at once pregnant and suggestive.

"That which moves us chiefly to speak of it in a moralizing vein
and as furnishing matter for serious reflection, is its large, liberal and
catholic spirit, and the contrast which it affords to anything which has
been done—or that could possibly have been done—by any Northern
writer.

"There does not appear anywhere the slightest purpose to preach a
sermon. The reader is led irresistibly to sympathize with the *Puritan,*

and, in some sort, to feel that the *Cavalier*, however noble and brave, is constantly putting himself in the wrong.

"This is entirely true to the theme. It is so natural, so logical, so inevitable as to pass unchallenged by the acutest Southern sensibility. In his allegiance to his art Mr. De Leon sacrifices no part of his loyalty to his blood and birth. The moral of his writing is entirely just and sound. But the fact remains—and it is this which is noteworthy—that our interest centers in a Northern rather than in a Southern group; and that, as for the author, we lose all trace of his identity.

"He might be a Tolstoi, or a Turgeneff, if a Russian could be suspected of knowing so much of our inner life. He might be a George Sand, or an Alphonse Daudet, his work is so deft and his personality so withdrawn. He does not appear as a Southerner at all, and he could not be a Northerner."

Such acceptance of this absolute truth to American character—on both sides of the supposititious "bloody chasm"—was general with the press of the whole country. Added to it was equal endorsement of the truth to local color and to incident, in description of novel scenes, actions and events, in a section still veiled to the eyes of a large class of readers. This latter feeling found, and still is finding, expression in hundreds of personal letters to the author and to the publishers of the present sequel romance, who had issued other of Mr. De Leon's writings.

Most of these letters were queries as to the ultimate fate of the *Creole*, of the *Puritan*, and of other characters who had become to their writers rather actual personalities than mere children of fiction.

For the double purpose of answering all these querists at once—and equally of giving fresher photographs of Southern character and Southern scenes, in some *unique* and hitherto untouched regards of both—the present romance was written. It will be found a continuation of the same train of thought; born of the same motives which drew so much commendation to the former book; even while wholly independent of that and a completely rounded story in itself.

THE GOSSIP PRINTING CO.

MOBILE, ALA., July, 1891.

# CONTENTS

# The Puritan's Daughter.

## CHAPTER I.

### ON THE GULF COAST.

The golden lances of a Gulf sunset shot almost level to the smooth bay, glancing from its mirrored blue only to be lost in low dimness of the opposite Eastern Shore; or to shatter into splintered shimmer against the bold, yellow bluff of Montrose, towering as solitary sentinel above surrounding flats.

There had been a thunderstorm since noon, that rolled away southwestward; but thin stretches of dun cloud, bordered with pink-edged grays, hung low over the west, barbetting as it were those light batteries, that hailed glinting fire from behind them. And now, the bloated face of the sun—all ruddier from contrast—stooped low to the very lips of the tree-purpled horizon, ready to command, "Cease firing!"

Out over the broad, blue bosom of the bay hung a dreamy, purplish-gray haze; far off, veiling the open Gulf, suggested here and there by bellying sails of great ships and flat-streaming smoke of tugs gliding seaward; —nearer inland, pulsing under reflected western glow, that tinted up above the Eastern Shore into streaked gleams of rose and lake and pink, vying in softness with the pearl shell.

And lower still, behind the marshes of that side,

began to broaden that pale, silvery gleam, here presaging the sudden rise of the full moon.

The scents of Southern summer hung heavy in the air; pine freshness, gum odors and breath of shrub all overcome, as the soft Gulf breeze stole on toward the night, by broad dominance of the magnolia grandiflora, starring through varnished gloss of leaf, as crown of triumph for some moss-draped giant in this " Garden of the Gods."

All was stillness and peace along the low western curves of bay-shore. Bordering this, its famous shell road wound like a steely serpent along its tree-dimmed length; only the plaint of the whippoor-will, or boom of meditative crane, hinting of any life beyond the low lines of white tents just inland.

These stretched away westward, in endless-seeming streets, angular, prim and white as blonde spinsterhood. But over the great city of canvas, the broad National flag clung listlessly to its peeled-pine staff, in the light breeze; and the stillness was as deep and strange as that, when the spectral host beleaguered the walls of Prague. Save at the extreme left, far toward sunset, not a soldier was to be seen on the great level plain, sufficient to camp an army. There, scattered companies had taken camp, at broken intervals; some hundreds of men, perhaps. But the lack of closer contact, aided by quieting influence of clime and hour, stilled the ordinary hum of evening camp; and, even about the mess-fires now glowing red, cooking progressed as silently as briskly.

Away eastward—close skirting the shell road and arched by interlocked arms of moss-clad magnolias and giant water-oaks—lay a long line of wall-tents. Floored

and with ample galleries under their spreading flys,
these were furnished with luxurious mockery of cam-
paigning hardship; and, advanced central from the
double line, the largest and best-appointed spoke " Headquarters" unmistakably, without the prompting of the
flag-sockets on either side of its low portico. On this,
in full enjoyment of the *dolce far niente* suggested by
hour and duty done, lounged a group of officers in
undress; various in garb to the casual glance; even
more so, to close observation, in feature, port and accent.

For this was the eve of the first experimental "Inter-
state Encampment;" the origin of that series which,
perhaps, did more to bring the soldiers of peace into
closer union and better understanding of their relation
to each other, than could have all efforts of the press, of
the Adjutant-General's office, of congressional enact-
ment; than could have done all other things beside,
save possibly a foreign war.

"How many men are in camp, Colonel?" lazily
queried a bronzed soldier, in semi-military riding dress,
as he stretched a pair of peculiarly small boots out com-
fortably before him.

" Three hundred and ninety-seven, at roll-call, General," crisply replied the officer addressed. "But the
Texans arrive at midnight, the Georgians and Caro-
linians by reveillé; and the Kentucky and Tennessee
troops at 9:00 A. M. We will turn out eighteen hundred
and seventy-six men "—this in half-query to the officer
on the settee beside him—" to receive the General and
the Northwestern brigade. No, never mind your roster,
Colonel Clarke. Do not rise; I am pretty sure of the
figures."

"By Jove! Colonel Winston, you always seem to be. Saving your eagles, there's a splendid sergeant-major spoiled by your rank!" laughed the one first addressed as general.

"I was that, at school, before I was suddenly promoted to private in the field," Winston answered, in his suave, courteous tone that still had the ring of command in it. "You know I am a lawyer, General, and we make our success by figures."

No stronger contrast showed in that varying group than between the two speakers. The General, far above average height, strongly knit and muscular, showed languid grace in every movement; yet with something telling of latent nerve and quickness that would answer, at need, as spark answers the flint-struck steel. His olive face, dark tanned, yet clear, showed no furrow in its rather long oval, while the drooping mustache had but two or three silver threads, and the close-cut, glossy black hair was touched only about the temples by Time's powder-puff. The long, muscular limbs tapered delicately, the tanned hands were small, but firm and nervous, with something feline in their action; while the feet, not too short, were slim and high-arched beyond the ordinary. Unmistakably of that Franco-Latin blood, still so common in the whole Gulf region, the man spoke wholly without accent or flatness; with the roundness of one who has used many tongues.

Colonel Winston, shorter by some inches, was still a tall man, well-built on rather lighter lines; agile, quick and nervous as a panther. Clear and sharply-cut features and keen gray eyes were softened by the winning smile frequent to his lips so firm in repression; and though evidently the younger man, his hair and mustache were snow-sprinkled; and Time, the champion, had left print of his knuckles from more than one "facer," during that endless and very "light glove" contest, we call life.

"You went in pretty young, did you not?" the General queried simply, removing his cigar and watching the lazy, upward curl of smoke.

"Seventeen," Winston responded, briefly. "Just the age I believe, Major Flint, that you played truant from the Iowa university to join General Buell's field-school."

"Seventeen when I went in, Colonel," the Northern soldier answered cheerily. "But I thought I was fifty before I got my company; and ninety before poor Lane and Harris answered the final roll, and I led the regiment to the sea with Sherman. By the way, Colonel, weren't you hit at Shiloh?"

"Yes; but I don't think you were the fellow that knocked me over, Major," Winston replied, with a laugh. "But we have you here, now, and as soon as General Everett arrives, I'll petition for a court of inquiry."

"Good enough!" laughed back the Iowan. "But I claim that you shall detail as judges some of those charming Southern girls you introduced me to at the moonlight concert last night."

"Detail considered made; prisoner condemned for life!" Winston chaffed back. "But, *a propos* of moons, look yonder!" He pointed to the eastern shore of the bay. "Let us stroll out on the wharf for moonrise."

The whole party rose and sauntered slowly out of the

camp-enclosure, toward the planked pier, running half a mile seaward and dotted with bath-houses prepared for the inland visitors to come. Winston and the General led the way; the others following in pairs.

" Who is the General?" Major Flint queried of the young Alabama officer walking with him.

" Didn't you learn?" the other replied. " Why, that is General Adrien Latour, a great traveler and one of the most dashing cavalry leaders we had. He was a Major-General at twenty-four. * After the war, he went into the Egyptian service as a Pacha, or something; and since resigning that has been all over the world."

" Well, by jingo! I should think he had seen enough of the real thing to make our play at it pretty dull for him," the Westerner answered, drily.

" How about yourself, Major?" the youngster retorted. " They tell me you went into the real thing pretty young, but you seem to be in ' the play' still."

" Oh, it is a matter of duty with me," Flint replied. " The guard is ' a big thing' up with us, and helps a man in a hundred ways. But down here you fellows go in for pleasure, fancy work and points."

" Maybe so," the Alabamian answered, with some pride. " And we get medals and blue ribbons when we carry the points away from home. But General Latour is not a guardsman, only a guest at headquarters. He and General Everett were classmates at the Point, and,

---

*Some swift critics of " Creole and Puritan " scouted a similar statement in that novel. In cold historic fact, General P. M. B. Young, of Georgia—later in Congress from that State and afterward U. S. Consul-General in Russia—left West Point a year before graduation; came South and accepted the adjutancy of Cobb's Legion, in 1861. He soon won his regiment; was promoted to his brigade for gallantry; and received his commission as Major-General, when he was scarcely twenty-four years old.

as soon as we offered him the command here, he tele-graphed Latour to come from New Orleans, as chief-of-staff. He declined, though; said he'd rather act as a courier. He's a wonderful rider, they say."

Their talk was broken in upon by the clear, rich tones of the man discussed, calling back:

"Major Flint, do they give you moons like that out in Iowa?"

"Not over water like that, General," the Iowan answered. "I have never seen anything like that line of light."

"What a lady friend of mine calls 'the moon-glade.' It is prettier than any landscape-painter could make it," Latour replied, slowly. "I have watched the moon rise over a dozen seas, but never saw a softer picture in silver than this."

## CHAPTER II.

### IN CUPID'S GRAMMAR.

THE group of officers, strolling leisurely under the arm-locked trees, had reached the main avenue, when a horseman galloped in from the shell road and drew rein as Winston approached. Tall and well formed, he rode with the short stirrups and heavy hand foreign to the South, and, without his blue regulation uniform, he had been spoken a visitor by the badge upon his breast —a ribbon halved diagonally in blue and grey, with the legend, "Northwestern Brigade," in plain gilt. And the face of the boy, for he was scarce more, had told his birthplace, even without the badge. Fair, broad and ruddy, with that healthful bloom born of Eastern fog, its oval was firm-based on strong slant of under-jaw; and the lips, rather thin for boyhood, set together in line firm enough to suggest a sternness, instantly dispelled by the frank blue eyes, which yet held little of merriment in them.

Dismounting quickly, but without the ease of the practised horseman, the young soldier saluted formally as Winston halted.

"Any fresh despatches, Captain Cushing?" the latter asked as mere form, quickly adding: "But I supposed you would stay in town and take the special at dawn, to meet the General's decorated train."

"I have despatches," the younger man answered, "from General Everett, dated at Corinth. All the party, the brigade"— he corrected himself with needless haste and more unnecessary blush—" is well, and will arrive on time. No, Colonel "—and again the pink complexion deepened visibly in the evening glow—" I did not stay, as you said there *might* be duty for me in camp."

"Did I? That was thoughtless of me," the Southerner replied. "You might as well have gone to meet the General and his family."

"That was not so important as duty, sir," the young man answered rather stiffly, but with another blush. "I will report in person to the General at the train. If you have no further orders—"

"None, Captain," Winston interrupted, suavely. "But I wish to present you to an old friend of General Everett and his family. General Latour—Captain Spofford Cushing, of Massachusetts; aide-de-camp to our commandant."

"Then you are my ranking officer, Captain," the Creole answered pleasantly, extending his hand. "But you must waive rank, though I am only the General's courier. I must shake hands with all his friends."

"Thanks; you are very good!" the boy cried, with a gratified smile, as he tore off his heavy gauntlet and grasped the veteran's slim, brown hand in his fair, soft and large one. "I have heard the Everetts talk of you so much, I was quite wild to meet you! Delighted, I'm sure, General! And she always speaks of you as Uncle Ad!"

"Oh, yes, Captain. Dalia—Miss Everett, you know, Colonel Winston—and I are great chums," Latour answered, with quick tact that ignored the personal pronoun Cushing used. "I dandled her on my knee as a

baby; and later sent her hideous dolls from Japan
And now, I honestly believe, my main reason for accep'
ing your courteous invitation here was curiosity to s
what ten years have done for the child."

"Child! If you could see Miss Dalia this minr
you'd smile at that term," young Cushing blurted (
"Why, in Washington, the way she met senators
diplomats always made me feel that I was only an ;
ward boy!"

"Indeed? She must have great *aplomb*," the
man answered, from behind a cloud of smoke.

"You will join our stroll out on the pier, Cap'
Winston queried, quickly.

"Thanks; I think not," the youth answere
some hesitancy—"I have duty—a—some letters
and to-morrow the General is sure to keep ;
With your permission, Colonel, I'll go to my t

"Only for the moment, I hope, Captain," Winston
answered courteously. "Come to headquarters after
taps, for a nightcap."

"Thank you very much," the New Englander answered, "but I never drink. I promised her—my
mother"—and again he grew very red—"years ago,
that I never would taste liquor."

"Deuced sensible promise, too," Latour broke in,
frankly. "I only wish I had made it at your age. But
come for a chat and a cigar."

"Thanks; but—you'll think me odd, perhaps—I do not
smoke, General. Good night," the boy added, hastily;
and, saluting, he threw himself to saddle and trotted into
the shadow of the trees.

"Nice boy, that," Latour remarked, vaguely, as he

took Winston's arm once more. "Rather raw, but a gentleman all through."

"He ought to be," Winston answered. "He represents one of the oldest names and largest fortunes in the Bay State. His father was in Congress when they became intimate with the Everetts; and the youngster volunteered on the General's staff, because he wanted to represent Massachusetts here."

"A most graceful resolve," returned Latour; "and influenced in part, perhaps, by a more rosy god than the son of Bellona. When a very young soldier's nomenclature makes a young lady 'she,' depend upon it Cupid is grammarian."

They had paused at the roadside to drink in the view beyond; themselves in the dense shadow of giant oaks and moss-draped magnolias. The round full moon hung over the eastern flats, glowing white as burnished silver and sending straight toward them, over the broad, blue bay, a fretwork of silver sheen, caught upon the little waves to be plashed into a million glinting sprays.

Over the whole East the vaulted blue gleamed cool and unbroken, while, behind them, the dying western light still glowed low above the horizon. One by one, twinkling stars peered out from the blue vault, blinked, disappeared an instant, only to return with stronger stare and looked steadily upon their own reflection in the water. Far away north, around the horse-shoe bend of shore, gleamed the city's lights, sole reminder of any handiwork save nature's. And the cool, soft night wind from the Gulf crept more boldly landward, laden with heavy sweets pilfered from tree and shrub; from that rarely rich night-blooming jasmine, prudish of perfume by day, but a very prodigal when wooed by the night wind.

"Let us go out on the pier, the breeze is fresher there," Colonel Winston said, at last. "Listen!" he added suddenly, as the sound of distant hoofs struck his ear. "That must be a courier from town."

"Scarcely; I hear several horses," Latour replied, after a pause. "And there are calls and merry laughter of women's voices."

The clatter of hoofs in rapid stride came nearer, and soon a party of six riders galloped around the curve, drew out of the shadows of the trees, and pulled up as they reached the group of officers, now in the fast growing moonlight.

Leading the party rode a tall woman of magnificent figure, controlling a fretful thoroughbred with easy hand as it danced under the mock salute made by her riding-switch. Her escort was a round-faced, boyish fellow, cut English by his tailor and far less easy in saddle than the lady. Next rode a fair, graceful young blonde; a wide, flowing sash of orange and blue, floating from the crossed-muskets on her shoulder and almost reaching her stirrup. Escort to her was a tall cavalry officer, now in fatigue, but with "Regular" stamped all over him, from cap to spur. Last came up a slight, girlish form, in faultless habit, followed by a man of square figure and heavy face, apparently saddest in the saddle, if his angled elbows and stiff knees told anything of truth.

The party drew rein, halting suddenly at motion of the leading lady's whip; and her sweet, bell-like voice called out, as Winston advanced from the group:

"Never mind the guard, Captain Prince! We're

only in mufti—I beg pardon," she interrupted herself—
"I thought the gentlemen were only some of our
boys."

"A mixed force, Miss Bella," Winston replied, with a
graceful bow; "and always ready to be your guard.
Howd'ye do, Robbie; enviable dog, as usual. Delighted
to see you, Miss Bessie; and, Captain Rumford, I
congratulate you on capturing the colors! Mrs. Smythe,
the camp is much honored; your charges must alight
and be the first to inspect headquarters—Mr. Smythe."
And the frank, courteous flow of welcome cooled a trifle
with that name. "General Latour, Colonel Clarke,
Major Flint"—he turned gracefully to the waiting group
—"let me present you to these friends, who compliment
us most by coming first."

Presentations made and names repeated, the foremost
girl leaned over her horse's neck; holding out a dainty
gauntlet cordially.

"We need no introduction, General Latour," she said
in her sweet, rich tone, "for we met in Paris."

"Why, I have not been in Paris"—the Creole's surprise began; but his *savior faire* promptly came to the
front and dressed on it, in such cadence as to hide any
break in the addition—"since that time!"

For ten long years·had passed since Latour had seen
the giddy city on the Seine; the girl before him in the
moonlight must have been a child then; and his trained
memory—usually so reliable for names—"fessed" here,
for once. But he took the dainty gauntlet frankly in
his slim, brown hand, as he added:

"And since then, Miss Moore, no surprise has been so
pleasant to me, as this."

"But I shall not grant even Bella's old lang syne a privilege I may not have, too," said the blonde girl, drawing off her gauntlet. "We are all so proud of your reputation, General Latour, that I want to shake hands, too."

"You are too good," the soldier answered, simply, as he stepped back and bowed over her hand. "It is well worth while to expatriate oneself, to be so welcomed home again. But let me second Colonel Winston's invitation, and urge you to dismount and 'sit beneath our tents,' as the Arab says."

"Are you in command until General Everett arrives," the blonde Miss Bessie asked, as Latour lifted her from saddle; leaving Miss Moore to Winston and Flint, while Mrs. Smythe sat quietly, until her lord dismounted, not without labor, and tugged her to terra firma.

"No, indeed," the Creole answered the little sponsor, with one of his rare smiles, as Captain Rumford promptly ranged upon her left. "I am only an aide, or courier, or something. Colonel Winston is in command, as chief-of-staff, and kindly leaves me off duty until the General arrives and assigns me."

Out of dense shadows had glided those small colored brethren, ever appearing gnome-like where there "is hosses to be holt;" and Mr. Smythe lagged behind the party, passing to headquarters, to give some final caution to the grinning little darkey nearest. The order was received with bared head; but the small groom grumbled to his partner in blackness:

"Tell'n *me* 'bout hold'n hosses! Guess *I* knows more'n 'bout hit'n enny man wot rides lak Moss Smife!"  ·

## CHAPTER III.

### OLD MEMORIES BY MOONLIGHT.

AT the tents, camp equipage was inspected, the beauty of the site gushed over; and Winston's man handed champagne around, apparently unbidden. Then Miss Moore fell easily into command.

"Light your cigars please, gentlemen," she said. "We did not come down to make martyrs of you. You were marching for the pier when we invaded you; so we'll let you take us, too. Will we not, Clara? You know, Captain Prince—it is not military, Colonel Clarke, but we always call Colonel Winston so, since he commanded our prize company—Mrs. Smythe kindly chaperones us. Shall we move on, Clara, dear?"

Mrs. Smythe took Winston's proffered arm, Flint obeying his signal and capturing Miss Brooke, the sponsor of B company; and Mr. Smythe, promptly counting himself number four, stepped to place and dressed on the regular who had joined Winston and his wife. Rumford still clung to the blue-sashed maiden, captured by the Iowan; and Miss Moore naturally dropped her hand on Latour's arm; taking the left of the line as they moved out toward the pier.

Miss Moore's cavalier was simply ubiquitous, flitting from group to group, the busiest of social bees. Fat beyond suspicion of angle, dressed to the latest verge of fashion, his beardless face had that rare faculty of perfect vacancy at rest, which may light into keen expression for a moment only to relapse as suddenly into dough. Robbie Pluffer was a known character in society; doing nothing, for business or for pleasure, yet a certain factor in every social affair. Seldom doing a wise thing, he rarely said a foolish one; save, perhaps, considering it bounden duty to "rush"—as he expressed it—every new-appearing star in his social firmament. Pleasantly tolerated at the clubs by younger men, one of their veterans had sapiently remarked: "Make no mistake about Robbie. He is only playing himself for a fool." Many a society knows such a youth; with eyes of tantalizing brightness and cheeks flagrantly smooth, who will be wholly boyish until fifty and then glide greasily and imperceptibly into "an old boy."

The moon had mounted higher in the star-studded canopy, flooding the whole scene with silvery-soft light. Under it, Latour glanced down with perplexed eyes on the face so near his shoulder. He had lived near neighbor to the Sphinx for years, but this handsomer modern riddle now puzzled him sorely.. Miss Moore's face was clear-cut, rather fair and wholly highbred. Her figure was superb, and she walked with that easy firmness which speaks character. She was not the style of woman a connoisseur forgets, but she looked twenty at most, and Latour had not been in Paris, as he said, for ten years. For once, the traveler failed utterly to recall a pretty woman's face or name. And now she was breaking the ice of long-lapsed acquaintance with the pick of platitude, talking in a sweet, rich voice strangely clear, and talking to the full as well as her subjects permitted.

" Those were delightful days in Paris," she said, suddenly, looking up at her tall companion with brown
eyes of fathomless depth. " You remember that day in
the *salon*, of course ?"

" You must not impugn my memory by suggesting
its loss of anything so pleasant," the man answered in
words. But he answered in thought: " Confound the
*salon !* Which and when was it ?"

" And —— the model ?" she queried, slowly, never
glancing up. " Was the resemblance accidental, or did
you find you had really known her people ?"

" Oh, merely accidental," he answered, easily enough ;
but his eyes left the fair face beside him to gaze out on
the moonlit water, deep memory darkening in them, as
the sudden touch of an old wound made him wince
inwardly.

A flood of recollection swept before him a scene in the
*salon* exhibition, at the Palais des Champs Elysées, ten
years before. He had chanced on an old Egyptian comrade, bear-leading an American party, the Moores
among them ; but he had exchanged no word with the
tall and rather awkward girl now so transformed.
Suddenly, out of a large canvas marked simply " A
portrait, Gerard, London, 1868, " eyes had looked into
his own, that dropped the color out of his bronzed
cheeks and carried him to the far-rolling Hudson—to
the first-love of cadet days ; to the parlor of a quiet villa
where he had trampled that love with cruel feet ; to desert sands, under just such a moon as this, whence the
supreme folly and sin of his life and all its sequelæ of
death, repentance and loss, had risen in bitter, mocking
mirage for years after. Before he had controlled his

emotion before that picture, the tall girl near him had said clearly, but so low none caught the words:

"So Colonel Latour knows the original?"

On his quick disclaimer of accidental likeness—no, it was a model he recalled at a friend's studio—the girl had answered with her lips, while the eyes underscored each word:

"The model has a face grand enough to impress somewhat even an old traveler. How awkward that Madonna's pose! Is it not, Colonel Latour?"

Strangely moved by memories of sin and suffering that dominated his usual tact, Adrien Latour had left the *salon* without reply, feeling, rather than seeing, the strange, deep eyes of that girl fastened on his face. Twice later, drawn by fascination of pain and remorse, the Creole had visited the gallery and paused before the face of Edith Van der Huysen, the woman who had loved and sinned, perchance had died, through him. And both times, as he turned away, had he noted Bella Moore's tall figure near him, though he believed he had avoided her notice.

Now, after all these years, and in the quiet moonlight of a Southern town, the sole spectre of Latour's past rose before him, summoned by the same voice. But Miss Moore, having quite broken her ice, cast aside reminiscence and the pick of platitude together; and now she talked with that mixture of brilliance and comradeship born only of tact wedded to experience. And the man, rapidly losing effort in real interest, met her sallies easily, and accepted her information with real respect.

The party had scattered about the piers and in groups.

Flint, in his direct way, was evidently interesting Mrs. Smythe with descriptions of Western life. Mr. Smythe, with his elbows well squared, and rolling his cigar between his lips, strolled restlessly toward them.

"This wind is too cool, Clara," he said, brusquely. "Besides it grows late and we'd better be getting a move on us!"

"Perhaps you are right," his wife answered, somewhat wearily. "Bella, Bessie! We must be thinking of our long ride home."

Flint again offered his arm; Mr. Smythe again ranged up alongside, with aggressive air of proprietorship; and, all that long wharf's length, bored the Iowan with the natural advantages of Mobile's harbor and that exceeding governmental parsimony toward it, which had lost him possible millions on investments. The others sauntered back in their old order; Latour—now all tact and ease—bringing up the rear with Bella Moore.

The silver disc hung high overhead, now; a flood of soft light on sea and shore even creeping under the tree shadows. The woman stopped suddenly and looked about her, as the low sigh of the night-wind whispered to the tree-tops and soft plash of frost-tipped waves seemed to murmur at the rough pier that barred their way.

"What glorious nights these are!" she exclaimed, with real feeling. "How much Nature has done for the South, General Latour! Each visit draws me to this section closer; makes me long more earnestly to live always in a land where——"

"Where mosquitoes are fiercest of the wild beasts, 'and only man is vile?'" he finished for her.

"Where manhood ripens and expands under your fervid sun, as it may not in our colder North!" the girl went on, gravely. "You know I am a Yankee, but in honoring your Southern manhood, with its rich heritage of glory and its grand endurance under trial—I yield to no Rebel girl among them all!"

"You are very good to feel so, and, of course, I feel that you are right," the Creole answered, rather sadly. "But I supposed 'Yankee' and 'Rebel' had been marked obsolete, in this day's lexicon of youth. I have been little in this country since the war, Miss Moore, but this rich feast of fraternity Colonel Winston is spreading for us would indicate reconstruction as universal as complete."

"But you take part in it," she retorted, quickly. "Why, if you do not believe in and feel it?"

The man glanced admiringly down on that flushed oval of cheek, so turned toward the Gulf that he could not question the eye, anent the tongue's sincerity. But he answered, quietly:

"I take part from basely selfish motives, I fear. As an event—pardon my dreadful want of patriotism—there is a trifle too much blue in it for eyes accustomed only to the gray. Doubtless you set me down as a military prig. I have not grown used to the color quite yet, and, but for Everett's urgence and the long interval since we met, I should not be here."

"I have always known you were uncompromising on this point, General," she answered, with the deft flattery of having followed his career. "Nor can I wonder at your loyalty for a cause that so delighted to honor you, almost in boyhood."

" I fear you are scarcely just to my prejudices, as they probably are," he answered, seriously. " They exist, not from the fact that the cause honored me too much, but because the irony of destiny has not made me honor that cause the less. But—" and another of his rare laughs rang out over the water—" we are beginning to talk politics, instead of sentiment, defying *Madame la Lune!* My gray hair must plead for my pardon, Miss Moore. We grow prosy as we grow old."

Bella Moore echoed his laugh with the bell-chime of her own, as she retorted :

" Be careful, General Latour! When you speak of being old it causes a twinge in your friends for the truth your face and manner assert so definitely. You have lived long enough in France to accept as fact that a man is only so old as he feels ; a woman, as she looks! "

" Taking your own theory,"—the Creole was all society man once more—" you speak most wisely for a little girl. "

Her brown eyes shot up at him, with quick, questioning gleam ; but the tanned face was calmly courteous and no light of chaffing shone in the black ones that met them so steadily.

" Unconscious satire cuts keenest," she half sighed. " That speech had been rosebuds and violets to dear little Bess yonder. But several seasons in society teach us that there are always thorns beneath the petals, and that violets live only as long as the butterfly of the Hydaspes. But "—she shot the query out suddenly— " you and he are very old friends ? "

" Dale ?—yes," he answered, rather to the magnetism than to the sequence of words. " We were room-mates at the Point, as boys; as men, we have been brothers across seas."

"He is a grand man!" Miss Moore dropped out slowly, as though to herself. "While he was senator, the Washington women haunted the galleries to look at him; and his rare speeches drew even me to hear them."

"So you do take an interest in politics?"

"No, but in some politicians, perhaps," she answered, brightly. "That is woman's way, you know. She often deludes herself that she glories in a cause, while really she only deifies its champions!"

"I never heard Dale speak," Latour said; a trifle too absently for strict acceptance of the lady's epigram. "He is a strong thinker. Does he speak well?"

"More than well!" Miss Moore promptly condoned lacking appreciation of her brilliance. "He carries his hearers on the flood of sincerity and truth that brooks no damming. Fancy a senator of the Union declaring Jeff Davis a great man, and General Lee the peer of Washington, under that dome!"

"And why not, pray?" the Creole queried, with a smile. "Mr. Blaine, who is the arch-type of party, glories in history; and the latter declaration is the dessicated truth of history!"

"Are many men brave enough to tell the truth"—she hesitated a moment; adding lower—"*always?*".

"With provocation—yes," Latour replied. He was buffeting the sentimental current that might float him into flirtation with this brilliant woman.

That she was of society, her ease and elegance left no doubt; that she was strikingly handsome, if not beautiful, the broad moonlight declared. Still, a nameless something seemed to him to rise between them; born, perhaps, of intuition, more probably of memory of that day he had faced his folly and his sin before the canvas of the *salon*.

And that nameless something made silence for awhile, that the woman did not break.

## CHAPTER IV.

### MENTAL PHOTOGRAPHY.

"I AM glad you like Everett's speeches," Latour said, after a pause.

"So does papa," Miss Moore replied, accepting the fiat of the nameless. "You know papa is a Republican —they would call him ' a horrid rad ' down here—yet he regretted General Everett's going out of politics, although a stalwart replaced him in the Senate. Mrs. Everett never cared much for Washington." This suddenly, almost abruptly.

"No; so she wrote me often," the man answered, innocently. "Odd, too; for she was devoted to society as a girl and, with wealth and the senatorial purple, there is no pleasanter place than Washington."

"None, indeed! It is *the* city of America," Miss Moore declared, with emphasis. "Mrs. Everett entertained as generously as graciously; but the quiet evenings I passed there, when the senate committees did not sit, showed me a home-life that explains her preference."

"And, besides, as her daughter grew up, Bennie felt the Washington influence bad for so young a girl," he responded. "Such a strange girl as Dalia must be, too, from their letters and hers. You know her, Miss Moore?"

"Remarkably well, for a society woman and a girl not yet out," she answered. "She is a strange girl, indeed, but wonderfully gifted. I do not mean to flatter her when I say she is her father's daughter. But you know her, General?"

"As a little child, yes," Latour replied. "I held her on my knee as a baby; fed her with a spoon as she toddled in at dessert a few years later; and saw her again the last time I was in the country. But ten years mean marvelous changes in your sex, Miss Moore, especially when they are changing the child into the woman. Is she pretty?"

"Not pretty one bit," she answered, frankly. "But handsome always; grand at times. At the piano, I have seen her Madonna-like; again, a Druid priestess, as the *motif* swayed her. Before her easel, I have seen her literally transfigured by a Joan-of-Arc glow, as she worked out one of her bizarre conceptions—not always true in coloring. On horseback, she is an Amazon; in her gymnasium, as nearly an athlete as a refined woman may be; in the home circle, a ray of broad sunshine."

"*Bref*, a juvenile female Admirable Crichton," Latour finished, with a laugh that had gratified cadence to it. "I'm rather glad that she isn't pretty, wholly so that she loves music, a grand refiner and a great resource."

"She not only loves it," Miss Moore said, warmly; "she has mastered it! She sings in lofty scorn of her own really rich and well-trained contralto, but her master in Boston—the best there—told her last year to go home and play! Time and the fullness of her own soul alone, he said, could teach her more."

"High praise that, for a girl not seventeen," the Creole controverted in perfunctory way. "As for her riding, that was born in her. Dale was the best horseman of his date."

" Saving one only," the woman answered, the brown eyes meeting his an instant only. But again he ignored the flattering implication that she had studied his career, and went on eagerly :

" Dear old Dale! your picture of his wife and child makes me comprehend better what his letters always say of home-life."

" And *you* are not married, General Latour ?"

There was pretty wonder in the rich voice, gracefully eager pose of surprise in the supple figure. But the quick ear that caught the one, the black eyes that flashed along the other, did not ignore the solecism.

Adrien Latour had known women of many kinds, under many skies. No trait of the fop touched his earnest, impulsive nature; and the bachelor of forty-six was still as unspoiled as had been the typical cadet of his date, or the woman-heroed junior of the generals of division. *Bon sang ne peut mentir* is more veracious than the average French proverb, and the stream in Latour's veins was too pure and far-reaching to be hastened by cheap flattery, or curdled by meretricious wiles.

He had sung and danced and flirted with the señoritas of the Southern demi-continent. In the far East, more than one mysterious figure, wrapped in her shrouding *abba*, had paused in passing long enough to whisper invitation from some great *khanum*. The stalwart horseman of her *Bois* had won the eye of lady and *cocotte* alike, in the giddy capital of the world. But, under all skies and ever at his elbow, stood the trusty Mentor, Self-Respect; and his errors, that may have been, were known to himself alone. Years gone, the Cairene coffee-houses had rung with his answer to one *abba*-wrapped emissary :

" Tell the *khanum* that smiles seem too cheap, which come unsought, to risk a bowstring for them. We *Giaours* would rather seek favors than stoop to lift those tossed us!"

So the traveler was no prig; yet his Creole *amour propre* was not wholly dulled by contact with the world; and the evident interest which this brilliant *mondaine* had taken in his career—and he an enemy to her section and an alien from his own—had not displeased him. But her last speech gave cold douche to what vanity he had. She was playing on him, plainly; and his answer went, as the pipe from Hamlet to the courtier:

" No; I am an old bachelor; and yet I have known women in a dozen countries."

But the little courtier in riding-habit did not pause to declare that "she could not play upon it." She simply ignored the wind-instrument, and returned calmly to the safer frets of friendship:

" And how eager you must be to meet the Everetts" —the pause threatened to grow awkward—"and they come to-morrow?"

" Yes, at noon, and on the great decorated train. Dale brings down a full brigade of Northerners of all arms; and they have an endless string of cars, growing as they pick up new commands. And Colonel Winston has planned a grand spectacle for you ladies and all the town," he added, as they reached the group about the impatient horses.

" He is right, Miss Bella," Winston added. " It will be a novel sight; and doubly a lesson of this country's military resources—every man a trained soldier at need;

equally of the real peace between men who fought each
other under that flag, who would fight for it together if
called upon!"

"Don't waste eloquence, Winston," Mr. Smythe said,
abruptly, as he lifted his wife to saddle and turned to
mount. "Don't spoil this moonlight by talk of fighting!"

"Assuredly not," Winston answered, with a suavity
that ignored the rudeness he replied to—"if the mere
mention of it troubles you, Mr. Smythe!"

"And O! Captain Prince," the sweet voice of Bessie
Brooke chimed in—"*will* you fight a sham battle?
Wouldn't *that* be lovely, Captain Rumford? especially if
my boys win, and then they'd be left in front of the
line!"

"No!—I protest, Sponsor Bessie," cried the young
lieutenant. "If that is all the glory B company is to
gain I'll throw over my chevrons and stick to my detail
on the staff!"

"Never mind him, Miss Bessie. I'll put him under
arrest for questioning your orders. Yes; the General is
right, Miss Bella," Winston added, as Latour assisted
the graceful woman to her seat, and her light hand controlled the impatient thoroughbred. "You shall have
the grandest parade the South has seen, headed by General Everett, a Union hero, surrounded by a staff of
blue-and-gray!" There was no suspicion of irony in
the tone that finished: "It will be pretty and peaceful
enough to delight you, Mr. Smythe "

There was pawing of hoofs and hubbub of adieux, as
Miss Moore leaned over to pat the arched neck of her
horse. No one else caught her low query to Latour:-

"*You* will ride on his staff?"

Not pausing for reply, she waved her whip, the bay mare sprang forward, and they clattered townward under a salvo of *au revoirs* ; as the officers sought the big tent and the box of " Henry Clays, " on its hospitable sideboard.

## CHAPTER V.

### BIOGRAPHIC—HISTORIC—PHILOSOPHIC.

"Who are the Smythes?" Latour queried, lazily, as the last officers strolled out of headquarters toward their own tents.

"Rather prominent society people," Winston replied. "Though he is not exactly one of —— us. He followed Sherman into Georgia, though not in a fighting capacity, I judge; brought some money with him, too. It was a useful commodity just then. He is shrewd, keen and close as wax, so he made more rapidly, went into insurance and moved to Mobile."

"But the lady seems to be of us?"

"Oh, yes. She comes of a great Carolina family, but they were poor as Job's traditional bird, and had the tastes of aristocrats. I presume it was a sale, but she seems content with the price. Monsieur is as jealous as Othello; madame is propriety itself. She spends what she chooses on horses, dress and bric-a-brac; ignores men more dangerous than Robbie Pluffer, and contents herself with striking us natives dumb on those pleasant occasions when we are permitted to see her china and plate and something of herself."

"Beauty and the beast," Latour answered, stretched at length on a settee. "But, if Beauty be content, *que voulez vous?* I tell you, Colonel, we are civilizing rapidly, eh? Our old, conservative towns used to hold to tradition closer than those busier communities of East and West, but your capitalized Progress is a wonderful leveller! I presume we need only to become equally as rich to grow equally as shoddy as the newest society in the land."

"I am afraid you are right," Winston replied, rather sadly. "Time was when the South gloried most in her traditions and clung to her motto, *Noblesse oblige.* Now that we are well entered in the race for progress, we have, perforce, given up mottoes for practicality."

"Rather say, changed our mottoes," Latour rejoined. "Now in the race for what you call progress—translatable cash—we flaunt only one society banner, inscribed, ' Devil take the hindmost.' It is fast coming to this, even in New Orleans, stronghold of Creole reserve. In my boyhood days, no American dared put his social nose across Canal street, though native and to the manner born. To-day, not to be American is a sort of reproach; and only last week a corn-fed plutocrat, from the far West, made me a plump offer for our old homestead."

"Which you resented, of course?"

"Oh, no. I merely looked at the man. I think the mild surprise in my gaze permeated even the few pores in his cuticle. *Mon dieu!* I really believe that had I chaffered, he would have made me a bid for the job-lot of old Latours and d'Auvignes on the walls."

"You are of the few fortunate ones, General," the Alabamian replied gravely. "Many would have been forced to—chaffer."

"*Tant pis pour moi!*" the Creole retorted frankly. "I often think that wealth is a misfortune for an old Confed. Were I forced to work for myself, doing so I should work for my people. That might solve the problem, so long a puzzle, whether there be really anything in me or not."

"Your old classmate solved that problem without the key of necessity," Winston said, rather bluntly. "When he went to the Senate, General Everett was a poor man."

"What made him rich?" Latour queried out of a cloud of smoke. "Character, New England pluck— northern climate! When Dale resigned that captaincy of engineers, with which his grateful government rewarded the services of its general of brigade, he had not a dollar. His acknowledged skill, the opportunities offered his clear foresight and Puritan common sense, by Northern development, made him rich. The well-won respect of his new statespeople in his Western home made him senator. Dale never was a trader or a politician. He is a legitimate result of inborn greatness."

"Aided by circumstance," Winston added decisively. "Had he been of us, surrounding had never given him opportunity for swift success. He might have been a senator, perhaps; but his resignation—or his counting out for a partisan contestant—would have sent him back to harder work, from contrast; unless he had chanced to become almoner for a life insurance company, or a— lottery!"

"*Peutetre!*" the Creole answered with a shrug. "But what could have induced him to accept a brigade of militia, I can not comprehend."

"He did not," Winston replied quietly. "His command is National Guard; the only standing army the government can rely on at need."

"Oh, I beg pardon," the veteran answered courteously. "Long absence has left me ignorant of the difference. But Dale always looked down on the volunteer service—mustangs, he used to call them—so naturally I wondered at his playing soldier, after he left the army."

"I do not," Winston said decisively. "Have you considered that it might not be play, but duty; that he took this brigade from the same motive that carried him to the Senate—principle? You have, as you say, General, been absent too much to grasp the minor changes *post bellum*. The Guard is our sole national reliance now; the bone as well as the muscle of the fighting nation's body. General Everett had been inconsistent to theorize for it in the Senate, but decline its practical working by refusing the command in his State."

"Do you not realize, Colonel," Latour answered seriously, "that we can not look at these matters alike? You have become an earnest citizen again, I am an alien. It does not affect results, if I be so from choice or necessity. You organize this fraternal feast of soldiery *a la* sauce of blue-and-gray; while for me, well, I am content to play courier to the Union general; or, beau to the pretty sponsor!"

"Consider the latter detail made, Private Latour!" laughed Winston—stepping with his rare facility from earnestness to suavity. "And now let me —— make you a toddy?"

"Ration accepted with almost equal thanks as detail," the Creole laughed back. "By the way, clever girl that Miss Moore. Who is she?"

The spoon, surprise-suspended in Winston's hand, ceased clinking his glass, as he stared at the questioner.

"Who is she? Why an old friend of yours, I thought. As soon as your coming was hinted, Bella Moore told Sally—Mrs. Winston; you'll meet her to-morrow at luncheon, General—that she was truly delighted; that she had known you in Paris; and—"

"Um—yes—certainly she did," Latour broke in quickly. "If she said we were friends, I shall never be ungallant enough to cry enemies! We *are* acquaintances of ten years' standing; though," he added drily, "I have not seen much of her lately."

"I was sure you were;" the now active toddy mixer replied, too busy measuring whisky to note the other's tone, "even had your meeting to-night been less cordial. Why she knows every detail about your career, your family and—my rather abrupt allusion to your bank account just now was based on her information to Sally.—How's that? Strong enough?"

"Quite strong enough; and sufficiently sweet for the occasion," Latour answered slowly; tasting the decoction, but thinking of the girl. "Did Miss Moore ask any particular questions about my past—the long ago?"

"No; she knew your career by heart."

"Flattering that; but you haven't answered my query. Who is she—when at home?"

"There she is a reigning belle of Washington," the Alabamian answered. "Here she is the guest and confidential friend of that dainty little Bessie Brooke, and almost as popular with all classes of society. She has been South several consecutive seasons—her father's gout, you remember; and she rather leads social matters among us, than follows them."

"Mother dead a long time," Latour said in that

neutral tone between query and assertion. And satis-
fied by the other's acquiescent nod, he added: "Odd;
but you find her sort in every country under the sun. I
mean, every country that rears Christian churches and
sends out missionaries for such as——I am!"

"By the way," Winston rejoined without noticing the
equivoque, "she must have been rather young when
you met in Paris?"

"They always are——" the Creole began absently;
adding hastily: "I mean her sort stay young always.
She was a grown woman then; she is a girl still. She
has grace, too; and tact *au bout des ongles.*

"Infinity of it," Winston rejoined warmly. "She is
the most graceful of women in a waltz, an argument or a
race, that the set can boast. Why the debutantes—and
she has fast friends in every succeeding group of them—
are as easy with her as the married set; she is the only
new girl Robbie never tried to rush; and yet there is no
effort about it all."

"No; there is nothing that might be called missyish
about her," Latour assented quietly. "She is a
thorough woman of society, but a very pleasant one;
and I am glad that she remembered our old—intimacy.
But, Colonel, you will have to wake very early, so I'll
let you turn in."

As if in answer to the suggestion, a tall black in undress jacket appeared at rear entrance of the tent,
and advanced to drop the portieres that divided the
spacious tent into reception and sleeping apartments.
They were the flags of the United States and of Alabama.

"Your cot is there, General," Winston said, with the
suavity of the practiced host. "I shall get out before

reveillé,to meet the Georgians, but need not disturb you —pleasant dreams." And he lifted the national flag as he spoke.

"Thanks!" Latour replied, as he raised his tall form from the settee. "But my conscience is so good—or bad—that I never dream. But—" he gazed half regretfully at the starred flag—"I scarcely expected that my bed-room draperies would be—that."

Winston looked steadily at the bronzed and handsome speaker as he said aloud :

"Not an unbecoming combination of colors, General, that flag of a great nation—*ours!*"

And, as he let fall the screening draperies, he added *sotto voce:*

"What bigots these Creoles always are. They are worse extremists than the Puritans themselves."

## CHAPTER VI.

### OLD FRIENDS AND NEW.

The Sabbath morning broke, as mornings of early summer break only in the Gulf region; cool, crisp and fresh, with dreamy, purpled haze hanging over the blue bay, and saltiness wafted citywards on the breath of a gentle south wind. Gradually the sun, lifting the mist-veil, asserted his supremacy of season, but before his rays had gilded more than the spires of Mobile's many churches and gables of her tallest houses, the quaint old city was astir upon the streets.

For the long-expected event was at hand and the "decorated train" would soon be due at the depot, that ended the broad, tree-embowered avenue of residences, running from two long miles westward to dip its feet in the river at the East. And, from that depot, the "Western brigade"—the first soldiers in blue to encamp upon Southern soil since the war closed—would take up its line of march for the camp of a new fraternity and peace.

Along its line of travel from its far away headquarters, this brigade had made one triumphal progress. Decorated with the flags of the Union and of the States whence came the several commands; draped with ever-greens and southern moss, and loaded with flowers, tendered by fair and bronzed hands alike, at every stopping-place; giving out joyous sounds of a dozen bands, its every stop was a frank and spontaneous ovation

direct from the hearts of the people, met as frankly by the
distant soldiery bent on new and far different conquest.

Echo of all this had preceded the expected train, and
now the masses in the streets, the belles and beaux at
the breakfast table, the very children bent Sunday-
schoolward, were excited, and eager for the great event
of that soft, sunny Sabbath. And none among the
throngs already massed " down town " were more intent
and eager than the negroes. Groups of neatly-dressed
men, their faces all ashine with perspiration and expectancy, escorted gaudily-dressed black females, blooming
out with odd-sorted and *voyant* colors, whether on showy
bonnet, typical " bandanna," ample-skirted dress or in-
herited kid gloves. But rarely among these happy,
laughing blacks now showed the traditional head-dress,
save where its flapping ends crowned some wrinkled
crone—relic of old slave days—who could not reconcile
herself to the new order of headgear. For the *post
bellum* Southern darkies, naturally as mimetic as the
Simian of the Indian jungle, ever ape the extremes of
what fashion they can see, glorying more in ill-fitting
cast-off finery of those whom they serve, than in neatness and comfort of new clothes within their reach.

As the sun rode higher overhead, the street crowds
grew denser, regardless of his rays, all sorts and condi-
tions of men and women filling available sidewalk
space; while balconies and windows of residences—filled
with eager-faced people of the better class—showed that
the interest in the Northern visitors was not confined to
one social stratum. Then couriers dashed about the
principal streets; while the regular drum tap sounded
on all sides, cut by occasional blare of brass and telling

of the massing of the escort of welcome. And at last, as the bells of churches clanged out to call sinful men to prayer, a group of officers headed by Colonel Winston trotted rapidly down Government street, amid shouts of recognition, or of welcome. For the home-soldier was ever a popular figure among his people, in uniform or without it; and behind him rode the best-known youth of the Gulf City, side by side with stranger guests from distant States—lately foes, but now friends come so far to shake hands across that supposititious " bloody chasm," which they could not find!

On Winston's right, controlling the colonel's pet mount with lightest-seeming hand and easy in saddle, spite of the powerful brute's restless curvet, Adrien Latour attracted every eye and query from every tongue. The plain gray jacket was innocent of braid or rank-mark; the plain black slouch bore no device or plume; but that quick intuition, peculiar to the *post bellum* Southern crowd, supplied all omissions and told all that a Confederate of name and note rode there, undistinguished save by port and bearing of a leader.

So the populace was not cheated. Hats waved, huzzas rang from the pavements, and more than one " tiger ! " threatened to run into the old-day " rebel yell; " while from balcony and window, handkerchiefs that fluttered and slender hands that waved at the little band especially singled out the gray — and now grim — rider.

" This is scarcely fair, Colonel," he said to Winston, as they passed a bevy of peculiarly demonstrative girls. " You said we would ride in quietly; and this thing is becoming a bore to me, if not to these gilded youth behind us."

"We are near the armory," Winston answered, with a graceful wave of his chapeau to groups on either side. "I think they really have detected the lion under your modest lamb's hide, General. It *is* becoming rather too much of an ovation, though."

"If they give his staff such a reception," Latour answered, with a gleam of white teeth under his mustache. "*Mon dieu!* what will they do when General Everett shows his army of love and loyalty! Your people are as impressionable as our Creoles—used to be!"

"Perhaps," Winston answered. "But many of them are too old fighters to let a jacket hide an old fighter from them—Halt!"

They drew rein suddenly, as a battery rumbled by, turned down the narrow street and wheeled into battery at its wharf's end; the gunners springing to place for the salute of welcome.

"Those fellows are soldiers," Latour said briefly; scanning the battery, as he sprang from saddle and threw the rein of his restive black to the ready orderly.

"They ought to be," Winston replied, with gratified smile. "They were the first company of my regiment reorganized at the reconstruction. Their battle-flag has fifty names upon it; most of the men were in the real thing, and their captain's proud Huguenot name had colonel before it when the end came. You see, General, it is not only 'us youth' who go into this playing soldier, as General Everett has done."

"*Mon ami*, you are truly an enthusiast," the Creole answered with a frank smile; but he drew his tall form to its full dignity as he saluted, and added—"and a soldier!"

The long scream of an engine from t      .h of town
was followed by the rumble of a h.      .ain; then
around a curve dashed into sight a           tive loaded
with wreaths, moss festoons and U :··  .gs, and, following it, an endless - seeming t··  ·.  Car after car
rolled by, each crowded with ʀ· ı`  decked with
evergreens and streamers, bearin· ·ɑɾ ι  and locality of
the command it carried; and, .·´  train came to a
stand, an imposing drum-majoʳ       ·ɡ to the platform,
quickly followed by a dozeɪ  ·.·  lothed bands, all
massing on the street.

As though by inspiration ·ɦ· ·ƈɑɪɪ of "Dixie" woke
wild-answering cheers froɪ ·ɕ· ·ɾong, redoubling as it
ran into " Yankee Doodle " ·ɑɪɪ· ·ɦen fell into the rhythm
of " Hail to the Chief." ·ᴵ··    the cars poured company, battalion and regi ·ɪ·   citizen soldiery; quick-
forming at the word   ·  mand, that cut through
murmur of comment ·ɪ´  · welcome, as each corps
moved into line and halted, " in place rest."   Discipline
quickly aligned that army of visitors, to the pleased surprise of the still larger army of curious gazers.

Into the parlor car, next following that of the band
and decorated with more flags, larger wreaths, and the
legend, "Headquarters Northwestern Brigade," Winston and Latour, followed by young Captain Cushing,
had sprung as the train stopped.  In its central aisle,
Dale Everett—ex-Union General, ex-Senator, and now
National guardsman—had rushed forward to lock in his
arms the late Major-General of Rebel cavalry!  And as
those stalwart men stood there—forgetting the past conflict and its sad sequelæ; recalling those early days of
the Point and boyhood's brotherhood—the glittering

4

group of peace soldiers about them felt that the war was indeed over; that its worst results were over and effectless, too!

When the Northerner at last released his brother-of-old, Latour turned to the section where the ladies sat, interested and expectant.

" Adrien !"—" Bennie !"

Only one word of greeting on either side, and the Creole had grasped Mrs. Everett's outstretched hand with a brother's clasp; then raised it to his lips with the deference and grace of a courtier. Nor had the keenest worldling, seeing their two faces, ever dreamed that to either of those true hearts the throb of passion had sent the blood of youth to fill it with hope, suffering, remorse; all to settle into the calm of highest friendship.

As General Everett released the Alabamian's hand from his cordial grasp of greeting, it was Latour's voice that said :

" Colonel Winston, let it be my privilege to present you to my dearest friends. Mrs. Everett, Miss Everett, this is our chief-of-staff here, my old war-comrade at Shiloh."

Then the fair and placid matron extended her hand cordially, adding :

" And our host, too, Adrien. We are no strangers, Colonel Winston. Your letters to my husband have made his wife and daughter your friends already."

" And I should know you best of all," Miss Everett said, as she turned from Latour's quick vocal questions, and the still more earnest query of his black eyes, to give Winston her ungloved hand. " I am papa's private secretary, Colonel; so I have known you longer than any of them."

## CHAPTER VII.

### A TYPICAL WELCOME

The hand the New England girl held out to the Southerner was white and shapely; but it was firm and steady; the fingers—not too long, but strong and tapering—closing on his with that frank pressure which has the force of character, as well as of muscle, in it. And the smile that accompanied her words showed white, even teeth, between lips somewhat too clear cut for perfect beauty, yet speaking will and power in every mobile curve.

Yet a casual observer had not, perhaps, called Dalia Everett a handsome girl. Under the clear, firm whiteness of her skin, the blood coursed in strong, healthful current that rested only an instant on cheek, brow and throat. Masses of fair brown hair were caught loosely back from the broad, white brow, shown by her sailor hat; and under it sparkled clear, blue-gray eyes, changeful in expression, but frank, direct and honest as those of a country boy. The nose, if a trifle too long for classic model, had thin, sensitive nostrils; and the tall, lithe figure carried its fair proportions with that ease which comes from the habitual exercise of healthy muscles, untrammeled by too much fashion, either in dress or pose.

As she stood there, in severely simple traveling dress, it is perhaps doubtful if the leader of a watering-place German would have pronounced Dalia Everett "a

doosid pretty girl!" But there is less doubt if any
average judge of women would have classed her as an
ordinary one; and the full, low tones of her voice—
showing no trace of accent and puzzling the hearer to
locate her birthplace—carried in them conviction that
this girl of seventeen always used that organ to say
something, when she spoke.

"But, my dear Dalia," Mrs. Everett said gently, "you
must let Colonel Winston present the General to a still
older friend than you claim to be." She turned to a
stately but still young and handsome woman beside her,
adding:

"Or let me—Mrs. Winston, this is General Adrien
Latour, one of my oldest friends and one of your brav-
est soldiers in those days when he and Dale were both
fighting for their principles."

And Mrs. Winston, who had gone out on the early
special to meet the Northern ladies, greeted Latour as
one whose name was historic, and welcomed him to the
camp of fraternity. Then she presented her escort:

"Major Beaumont, General Everett's aide, whom I
will not really consent to relieve as my chief-of-staff,"
she said, with her singularly sweet smile.

The gentleman so indicated advanced with easy grace,
that hinted little of his three-score-and-seven years, and
grasped the Creole's hand warmly.

"Of course I know General Latour," he said, simply,
"although we never met during the last war. But
your father and I fought together under Harney in
Florida, sir; and we rode side by side through the
Belen gate behind General Scott. I believe we both
serve on the staff here?"

"Perhaps, unless Bennie—Mrs. Everett takes me as her chief-of-staff and Miss Dalia's," the Creole answered. "And I am truly delighted to meet you, Major Beaumont, as my father's old friend, who will make a new one of his son."

"He could be nothing else," was the response, with an old-time bow, "since my old comrade's best traits have been so illustrated by him."

Type of that old school so fast disappearing under the hot progress of to-day, Major Beaumont was tall and dignified; courtly in address to man, as to woman, but ever showing gleams of genial, sunny nature under the somewhat florid graces of a generation gone. One of the first to volunteer to General Jackson, when the horrors of the With-le-coo-che massacre sent the flower of Southwestern youth to Florida, rifle in hand, the Major had won his rank under Worth, in Mexico; and had worn it gallantly in the conflict between the States. But he clung with the fervor of a first love to that old company whose rifle he had carried half a century before; and now, heading its honorary roll, was the most popular and energetic member; and the proudest of the national repute for drill and discipline of " his boys." A widower and grandfather; of easy means and a scholar from taste, the Major was the most sought beau of the most petted belles, and offered his *bons-bons* and *bons-mots* with the grace of a Grandison, tempered by the manhood of a Colonel Newcome. Sadly rare grow these specimens of the truly " good old days," amid the whirl and glint of to-day; yet all the more refreshing to the just sense, wearied by the newer, if not nicer, order of things social.

And it was the old Major who suggested:

"But we must not cheat the public of its pageant longer, Prince, if the General is ready."

"Certainly not, Major," Winston answered, tightening his sword-belt and inwardly coming to "attention." "Sally, you will take charge of the ladies until we join you after the parade. General, if your pleasure, I will ask General Latour to ride as chief-of-staff, while I command the escort."

"What, in this jacket?" Latour cried, with a laugh. "No, no! Colonel Winston. I suspected something like this when I *forgot* my stars and belt. If Major Beaumont will permit and Mrs. Winston consents—"

"You shall be his second in rank and act as our aide-de-camp," Dalia laughed. "Shall he not, mamma? Why, Spofford, you dreadful boy!" she interrupted herself, with hand cordially outstretched. "How dare you hide behind papa all this time, and not notice us poor, down-trodden womenkind?"

"I was on duty, Miss Dalia," Captain Cushing answered, quietly; but his fresh face took on sunset hue, as he added:

"I was not hiding, Miss Dalia."

"Read your book of chivalry, sir," Dalia answered, with a smile that belied mock-reproof in her tone. "The knight's first duty is to 'laydies fayre.' Mamma, here is Spofford. Mrs. Winston, let me present Captain Cushing, of Massachusetts. Major Beaumont, Captain Cushing, a veritable Yankee, like papa, who hopes to go to the 'Mayflower' when he dies."

"But would never have been content to die without seeing your beautiful section," the youth retorted, gracefully, to Mrs. Winston; his blush deepening as he added lower to Dalia: "And you were so occupied with new friends."

"Old friends are ever welcome," the girl answered, frankly. "Doubly so when one is among strangers, cordial as they may be. But, my!"—her mood changing quickly again—"what a grand new uniform you have! How well it looks."

"It *is* very well, thank you," the guardsman retorted in pique, "and we hope it finds you the same."

"Don't be a goose, Spofford! I knew you were well; you are never anything else," Miss Everett replied, in a motherly way. "You know mamma and I are delighted to see you; and now 'duty' is done, I suppose you will help escort us to see the parade."

"I regret that duty on the staff will prevent," Captain Cushing answered gravely; "besides, I heard General Latour promise to do so, and your party will be full. He seemed *very* anxious for your arrival when we met last night."

"Of course he was," the girl said, her frank eyes fixed on the Creole. "You know we have not seen Uncle Ad. for so long a time. But you'd better come, too. Major Beaumont"—this aloud—"there will be room in the carriages for you gentlemen?"

"Ample room," the veteran responded, with the same bow he had vouchsafed the Queen at her drawing room. "Colonel Winston is too true a soldier not to anticipate a lady's wishes."

"Mrs. Winston, not Upton, taught me those tactics," the Colonel answered, quickly retreating behind discipline and saluting, as he added: "Your horse is ready, General! The line is formed, sir!"

And glancing from the car window, they saw the brilliant staff already in saddle, and Captain Cushing somehow outside and clambering into his; while Adrien Latour's late mount, shining like black satin, reared at every change of arms and wrestled fiercely for the bit with his nimble orderly.

"Oh! isn't he grand! A perfect beauty!" Dalia cried, with her cheeks aglow. "How I should like to ride that black!"

"Or try to, perhaps, Dalia," Latour said, smiling. "No lady has ever mounted Jo. Johnston, the Colonel tells me; and my hands were pretty well occupied keeping him down, as we rode from camp."

"I will ride him if the Colonel will let me," the girl answered, quietly. "Now, see papa admire him—and see how he comes down!"

Winston and the General had left the car; the latter walking straight to the plunging black, taking in his points and temper at a glance, and laying a firm hand on his corded neck. The orderly gripped the bit-rings with both hands.

"Let his head go," Dale Everett said, quietly, as he gathered the reins in his firm hand; and the next instant he was in saddle and the black horse trotting toward the glittering line, on Winston's right, as thousands of muskets rattled to "present!" and the consolidated band thundered "Hail to the Chief."

The colors of twenty States dipped in salute, side by side; the old Southern battery sent its echoing volley out over the peaceful water that sunny Sabbath noon, and the suggestive pageant had begun.

# CHAPTER VIII.

## THE LEGIONS OF FRATERNITY.

"It is a beautiful sight!" Mrs. Winston cried in genuine enthusiasm, for her soldier had conceived and organized it.

"It is a very touching one," Bennie Everett answered warmly; and her eyes were misty as her fair hand rested on the Southern wife's and pressed it in the frankness of new-found friendship.

"It is a very meaning sight. The war is over, indeed!" The words came slowly, in the low, rich tones of the Northern General's daughter. Her eyes, fixed steadily on the long line, were full of earnest light; and the color rested in the fair cheeks, as she added simply: "We are but one nation after all!"

But Latour's eyes were not on the military show, brilliant though it was. They had a wondering query in them, as they rested steadily on Dalia's face; and his ears took in none of the sounds so prideful to the lordly drum-major. For those tones of the young girl summoned up a memory from the long-dead past, when he was but a boy by the Hudson; when another contralto, deeper but less sincere, had spoken strangely similar words. But he only said, and rather lightly:

"Those facts were finished before you were born, Dalia."

"In some sort, perhaps," the girl answered, never moving her eyes from dipping flags and changing arms.

"But papa always said, in speeches dictated to me, that the war would never be over, in actual fact — that prejudice and hostility of section could never cease — until the men of North and South, who had not fought, learned to understand each other by personal contact."

"As you and he understood one another, Adrien," the mother added, with frank eyes moving from her daughter to her old friend, "even when you had arms in your hands. Dalia is right, as her father has always been. This is peace."

"*Sed, inter arma non silent leges,*" misquoted Major Beaumont. "For see, Mrs. Everett, that is our excellent Mayor, ambushed in his council at the head of the column. Ah! he will capture the General, rescue or no rescue. Now Colonel Winston presents him, and he will present the freedom of the city, not in a golden box, as in London, but in most silvery speech."

"But he is merciful by nature," Mrs. Winston added, hopefully. "He will not make it long."

"Noble man! For I am crazy for a sight of your much-described city," Dalia exclaimed, skipping briskly from the woman back into the girl.

"Noble man!" echoed Latour, fervently. "For I confess to a weakness for lunch, Mrs. Winston, and that obdurate tyrant of yours had us breakfast at reveillé."

"And that more obdurate tyrant, his wife, will not let you escape lunch, just after parade, General Latour," the Mobile matron returned with matter-of-fact hospitality. "Only our little party here, strictly."

"And, meantime, my commander will order me to order an appetizer," Major Beaumont said. "And may I serve as acting commissary and issue Miss Dalia a ration?"

He produced a box of *bons-bons* from under the seat, handing them to the ladies as he made an unseen signal to a colored soldier, standing an ebony statue in the pantry door. Before the ladies had ceased exclaiming at the veteran's promptness, the statue, now animated, handed champagne cocktails, in tall, frost-rimmed glasses.

Quite as tall as the Creole, lithe and clean-limbed as a greyhound, ebony black, and neat to the verge of foppery, the man was in officer's regulation undress. He wore it with easy unconsciousness of habit, not that apish effort at imitation common to the colored soldier; and Latour's quick eye noted that the shoulders were eyeletted for straps, though he wore no rank marks.

"This is my own peculiar specialty," the courtly Major said, raising his glass with a caress, after handing the ladies, and indicating one to Latour. "Powdered ice, no sugar, a touch of vermuth and a thought of Angostura; two ripe berries and only the peel of lemon. Each one of these draws out the best qualities of champagne, as adversity does the nobility in man's nature. Mrs. Everett, Miss Dalia, son of my old comrade, welcome to our Gulf City!"

And the party sipped the restful mixture, with equal appreciation of the speech and the beverage.

"Splendid specimen of the man and brother, that," Latour remarked, as the servant strode out of ear-shot, with good stride and rhythm. "He recalls my old Jellab orderly at Cairo."

"But is he a real soldier, Major?" Dalia asked, with wondering eyes on the retreating black.

"Yes, and a real anomaly of our singular military system," the veteran answered. "Carter is a combination possible nowhere out of the cotton States; I had almost said, out of our own. He is captain of a crack colored organization attached to Winston's regiment; knows his military rights and political equality perfectly, but recognizes his social situation equally. At the head of his company, when inspected on muster, he expects and receives consideration; military equality, indeed. Muster done, he takes off his shoulder-straps and is a thoroughly capable and respectful servant."

"But he is in uniform?" Dalia queried in her insistent way of getting to the bottom of all things she took the least interest in.

"Yes, fatigue. But the colored troops take no part in the encampment, it being one purely of invitation; in fact, Carter had the tact to head a petition to the Colonel, that all colored soldiers be relieved from duty this week. So, being no soldier, he can become steward at headquarters, and many of his comrades find congenial and profitable work in camp."

"That is an anomaly," Miss Everett said. "I judge it is a very useful one to the colored men, too. But, is it exactly right?" The girl's face was grave, and her voice had serious vibrance in it.

"My dear little girl," Latour put in, "when you have lived as long as I have, and under as many changing skies, you will become quite as much of a Turk, in the quality of belief that whatever *is*, is right!"

"And, after all," Mrs. Everett answered, thoughtfully, "I do not see more moral wrong in this colored soldier's volunteering to do for profit what our regular privates are often eager to do on detail."

"You have reason, madame, as our French neighbors say," the Major returned, with a low bow. "For one, I am not too much democrat to rejoice in so much of caste, as precludes necessity to black my own boots. But, Mrs. Winston, your merciful Mayor is finishing. General, we must get the ladies to the carriages."

Under skilled tactics of the Major, the party was quickly at the proper club; and the ladies escorted to the seats reserved for them on its broad, and already crowded, gallery. Several groups of pretty girls, wearing the colors of companies that had chosen them as sponsors and maids of honor for the coming competitive drills, were soon introduced. Southern cordiality brought others, of both sexes, for presentation; and the Everetts were holding a small levee, as the head of the military pageant of fraternity swung into sight, following its consolidated band of over one hundred.

And a grand and blood-quickening sight it was, even to a race less impulsive than those Southrons of the Gulf Coast.

At its head rode General Everett; Winston at his left and a glittering staff behind, composed of home and visiting officers; all of them guardsmen of note, and many who had entered their profession under matriculation of fire. Then came the cavalry escort; the men riding with the dropped toe of Southern horsemanship, but the hands falling easily and every horse shining in the sun, from careful grooming. Next rumbled on battery after battery. various in uniform as in form and feat-

ure of the men; for the North and far West had sent
their best gunners to compete with those of the noted,
but yet unknown, Southland.

Lastly swung by battalion after battalion—regiment
after regiment, of the picked infantry of a dozen
States; the Southerners marching as the escort to the
Northwestern brigade.

Vigorous, easy and well-appointed, the men from the
colder climate marched, under the now hot sunshine,
with steady step and good cadence; their eyes held
straight front by supreme discipline, that overmastered
even curiosity at the new sights, of which they had
heard so much; or that still more tempting array of
beauty they felt, without seeing, was sending admiring
glances down, with its murmurs and applause and wav-
ing fans and flowers.

On in steady stream pressed the massed army of
peace, swinging around the club corner and giving good
view of its somewhat varying wheel; the light, long
swing of the Southern boys, accentuating the steady, if
less rythmic, step of the Western men. And, together,
that brigade told—if none other and more deep—a true
story of that reliance which the wide-reaching Republic
might well place in those ever-ready reserves, that could
practically leave the standing army but a skeleton in
peace.

And at the column head—lifting his chapeau as the
vivas broke out afresh, and smiling his grave, contented smile—Dale Everett sat his dancing, gallant
black, as though horse and rider had known none but
each other; leaving behind him fresh-renewed cheers for
the soldier of the Union who had proved so generous a

foe in war, such a stanch defender of the South in all her dark drama of reconstruction!

"It *is* a grand sight! Better than that, as you said, a touching one," Mrs. Winston exclaimed, and her plump, dimpled hand crept to the one in Bennie's lap. "I do not know, dear Mrs. Everett, how we can thank the General sufficiently for coming."

"And for bringing with him those whom the true soldier most delights to honor," the Major added. "You are right, Mrs. Winston. It is a touching sight, the foes of yesterday shoulder to shoulder to-day."

"Allowing for imagination," Latour whispered over Dalia's shoulder. "For it seems to me that if most of those marching gentlemen were foes in the war, their weapons must have been teething-corals and pap-spoons!"

"Fie! Uncle Ad!" the girl laughed back. "Can't you forgive them for not being as old as you and papa? *Didn't* he look grand, though? Did he ride like that at the head of his own brigade?"

"Not precisely, I judge," the Creole answered, flashing a quick smile at her earnestness. "But it is the happiest recollection of the war to me that I never saw the dear old boy that way."

"You both felt that dread!" Mrs. Everett turned quickly, catching his words. "I remember his telling me in New Orleans—"

She paused abruptly, a surge of color flooding her face. She recalled that in those days of New Orleans, close following the peace, both these men had been her lovers; that their swords had crossed—for the only time —through some strange mystery, as to her.

But, with all his reliant, inborn tact Adrien Latour extended his hand, as it were, to help her across the rough stones of remembrance her usually placid feet had strayed upon.

"But however your father rode, little girl,"—he was already answering Dalia—"he rode like the Bayard, 'without fear and without reproach.' This is the secret of his riding here to-day; that he was still true to his flag, while he never forgot to be true to himself!"

"Your father is almost as well loved in the South as are our own heroes, Miss Dalia," Mrs. Winston said in her sweet, frank way.

"Our section became his debtor during the war," added the Major, gravely. "He has forced usurious interest of gratitude upon us since, by his public life."

"*Bref!*" Latour chimed in with rare enthusiasm. "He is a true king Arthur, if in the lists, or at the Table Round!"

"And you are his Launcelot, Uncle Ad!—no—no! Perhaps you are his equal in prowess; but you would never misuse his trust—betray his love! Well, you are too old for a Galahad; but I should never call you—*my Launcelot!*"

The rich, low tones of the girl's voice vibrated on the man's memory, until it lost the present utterly, looking only into the past. He was a boy once more, upon the wide plain at West Point; a firm, soft hand pressed his; dark, glowing eyes read his own, as this same voice spoke those same words,——"Farewell, *my Launcelot!*"

For the second time that day, the voice of that young girl—fresh, natural, innocent as she was—conjured before his eyes a dark brunette of early days; she who had made him love and suffer and sin; she who had long expiated all by the last sacrifice!

The pageant—the present—the girl herself all dissolved from his sight, and, a moment, memory's mirage transformed the green park opposite into arid desert sand; the garish sunshine became the white moonlight, while under the shadow of the Memlook's minarets, he heard again that voice—silent in the grave before Dalia had ever spoken—echo out of the long-dead past:

"*My Launcelot! at last!*"

## CHAPTER IX.

### ON THE SHELL.

The lunch on Mrs. Winston's hospitable board had
just ended, after pleasant discussion of much-enjoyed
solids, which now drifted into that complaisant discussion of people and things ever induced in well-fed
humanity. And a merry but exceptionally charitable
group, it was, which Everett and his host had hastened
from the parade to join.

Succulent Gulf "reefers" had been served on thin
blocks of ice, spite the proverbial prohibition as to oysters in months that miss the "r." Small, salty and savory,
the little fellows clung to their black-tinted shell, which
lent their own complexion to the bivalve, with tenacity
far from hospitable. But, following Major Beaumont's
injunction: "Only a pinch of salt upon the heart, a
squeeze of lime-juice to send it through his system,"
the Northerners had found the proverb fallacious to
degree. Then came soft crabs; great, comely fellows,
cobweb-clad, that seemed to have shed their shells at the
very moment of touching the broiler, for delectation of
the strangers; and with them peeled tomatoes, blushing
in pale mayonnaise, as in shame at the nudity imposed by
one dip in boiling water, that stripped their jackets off.
There, too, were the famous crab omelets of the Gulf
coast, light and frothy as a *souffle*, but permeated with
the very soul of the unseen crustacean. And the Major,
happy in his cunning of the commissariat, dilated on

the proper use of beverages; brewing a tiny arrak-vermuth cocktail as appetizer, and pointing why the claret should be reserved for the omelet, while the white wine of France, directly imported, was the only true vehicle for the delicate flavor of the "reefers" and soft crabs.

"I have eaten oysters everywhere, my dear Madam," he said gravely to Bennie, "but none equal those of our Gulf City. The mammoths of Northern waters can not compare to them, having perhaps the same modicum of flavor to permeate ten times the mass of tissue. Baltimore boasts of her ladies first, her bivalves next. If we only equal her in the first, we certainly excel her in the other. And these are not plants, but merely 'native here and to the manner born.' As for the Britisher's 'natives,' they are what these tiny fellows would be, were they boiled with copper cents! It may surprise you, General, but they eat Mobile oysters not only in Chicago and St. Louis, but in Duluth and Salt Lake City."

"If you pass me the limes, Major," Latour broke in, "I will swear that they are the very best missionaries we can send to the Mormon."

Next came the lordly pompano—sovereign *de jure* of all the finny realm of the Mexican Gulf; and with this, the veteran lieutenant of Lucullus permitted beakers of Roderer, the champagne most affected by connoisseurs of this section. Delicate solids followed; the end crowned with late strawberries, delayed, the Major said, in special compliment to Miss Dalia. And he taught the strangers their novel service, by eschewing cream and all else save the juice of a ripe Florida orange squeezed over them.

And now, as they sipped amber-clear coffee from tiny cups, Winston asserted his special right to make the *chasse-cafe*, concocted of a dozen cordials and *liqueurs—* each resting upon, but never tinting the contrasted color of its neighbor—and served in tissue glasses, tall and thin-shanked as dyspeptic youths of fashion.

"Light your cigars," Mrs. Winston said to the gentlemen. "I must speed the parting guest too soon—There, the signal already!" she interrupted herself, as a cannon boomed out clearly from the wharf.

Over the entire route of march, the peaceful army of occupation had red-lettered that Sunday in Gulf City calendar. Welcome, heart-born and earnest, had met it on every hand and from all classes and colors, for on his breast every man of the Northwestern Brigade wore the badge, halved in blue and gray; and, under the flag of re-cemented nation, shoulder to shoulder marched the men, and the sons of the men, who had fought for, or against, it of yore, each by his light and each believing he was right.

And then, still followed by the roar of friendly thousands, the brigade and its home escort had marched back to its decorated train, had embarked amid bellowing guns, screaming whistles and fresh cheers, to whirl away to its camp under the magnolias.

And now, lunch over and carriages and mounts in waiting at the door, Everett was ready to follow his brigade and assume formal command for the week's exercises.

Suddenly these carriages moved aside, as a coupe

dashed to the door, and one gentleman, quickly followed
by another, sprang out to assist two ladies to alight.

" We did not stand on ceremony, Mrs. Winston," Mrs.
Smythe said, very cordially, as she ran up the steps,
" for we wished to be presented to Mrs. Everett and
claim her, before we were forestalled."

" And I begged to come on her staff, that I might
renew an old friendship, under skies I almost claim as
my own!" Miss Bella Moore's voice was pitched in its
most sympathetic key now, as she advanced to kiss Mrs.
Everett, with somewhat perfunctory effusion ; embraced
Dalia warmly and extended a dainty glove to Everett
himself. Then she fell back with pretty tact, to leave
the field to Mrs. Smythe, for introduction of Robbie
Pluffer and her omnipresent spouse. This, followed by
that lady's graceful urgence "for one day, at least,"
well-masked the dangerous battery of Miss Moore's
eyes—supported by the rich contralto that said, only
loud enough to be heard by Latour :

" Why were you selfish enough to spoil the parade—
for your friends. Clara and I avoided the clubs and
watched for you from her gallery. You let *us* expect
you. Was it laziness or—— "

" The military tailor," he finished for her; not
without a meeting of the black eyes and the brown.
" I told you I was Dale's courier; but now I have been
promoted to Bennie's commissary."

" And Dalia's ?" The woman spoke quickly; just a
shade of irony in her tone, hid by the changed voice
that added sweetly : " I feel you were the gainer, by the
loss to other—friends; for Sally is a dear hostess and
just the safest of chaperones. Besides, I hear that the

club gallery was a perfect bower of beauty, even to a
traveler like you, General.  Still, I had promised the
girls on our gallery that they should see you—all—ride
by; and bitter were the reproaches *your* desertion
heaped upon my head!"

Again Miss Moore's eyes underscored the mere con-
ventions her tongue framed; but the man was spared
reply, in either way, by Mrs. Smythe turning to him:

"Oh, yes; General Latour and I are old friends," she
was saying—"twelve hours old in person, but almost
always in memory of his past, on my part.  And as the
rigors of war will not let you come to us, for dinner, on
Wednesday, we will invade and capture you all on
Thursday, for a picnic lunch at Dog River.  You ride,
Miss Everett?"

"Papa would disown me, did I not," Dalia answered.
"I am his proudest pupil and he was the best horseman in the army."

"Was he?" Latour broke in.  "Very well, Miss
Everett, then some one else may carry you cross country
this week and teach you these intricate Gulf woods!"

"You vain old man!" the girl laughed back—"I
meant in *our* army."

"*Væ Victis!*" he retorted.  "I presume, like Mr.
Eugene Aram, I can not ride 'with gyves upon my wrist.'
Mrs. Smythe, if this picnic be yours, the head of your
slave and his horse are at your disposal."

Mr. Smythe shot at his *cara sposa* a glance that had
two-and-a-half per cent. of command in it; and she,
ignoring its existence with infinite tact, carried out its
spirit with equal precision.

"I accept the proffer with all its responsibilities,"

she answered gracefully, "and will assign you for safe custody to Bella—Miss Moore."

"Thank you, dear," that maiden responded, warmly, to Mrs. Smythe, but at Latour, adding promptly:

"But we are detaining these dread disciplinarians, Clara dear, and they pine for war's alarums down the road."

Adieux were spoken. Mr. Pluffer shook hands from the elbow with all the ladies, bestowed a grave bow upon each gentleman, and turned finally to Dalia, on the front steps:

"Mrs. Smythe is goodness itself," he said, blandly. "She has promised me the honor of being your escort on Thursday." And he faced to the right at the carriage door and handed the ladies in.

Five minutes later the other party was bowling down the road, coming around a sudden turn at Frascati in full view of th efamous shell road, Mobile's long-time boast.

Far away to the left, across a narrow strip of sandy flats, spread the broad bay, losing itself southward in the dim and distant Gulf of Mexico. Blue, calm and scarce rippled by the south breeze, the water lay like a huge turquoise, in setting of soft, purplish haze that veiled the lines of the distant Eastern Shore and softened the jutting points on the hither side into dreamy greens that made perfection of picture.

The road itself—giving back clear ring from the strident hoofs—wound around summer grounds and pleasuring places and stretched away south, under grand arches of magnolias and oaks, while giant pines stood out as sentinels with heads erect in the odor-laden air. Here and there showed rows of venerable cedars, gnarled and ragged, but ranged in avenues, reminiscent of passed home-grandeur of some progress-erased and forgotten old family. And about their trunks and lower limbs, as over all undergrowth and hedge that offered hold for its tendrils, twined the Cherokee rose, delicate and fragile, gemming the varied greens with those bluish-touched white stars, seen nowhere but along the Gulf coast.

On the right hand, close-skirting the drive and stretching far inland, lay rich farm and tasteful villa lands, broken into picturesque landscape by great, dim patches of untouched pine woods, needing only the hand of enterprise to denude them into doubly-productive richness. For about these, everywhere, gleamed the varied and practical greenery, suggesting the new-born gardening mania of the Gulf section.

Dalia lay back in the open carriage, with flushed cheeks and thirsty gaze, drinking in the novel beauty of the view, but silent for awhile. Then, with a deep sigh of pleasure, she exclaimed:

"It is simply perfect! Oh, Mrs. Winston, it was truly written that God made the country!"

"And, unfortunately with us down here," Latour finished for her, "it might end, and man left unmade the town."

"One need not want any towns in such a country as this," retorted the illogical sixteen, facing him in her decisive way. "But look, Mrs. Winston! Isn't he lovely?"

"Another effect of novelty, I fear, and somewhat aided by distance," Mrs. Winston replied, with one of her bright smiles. "He is racing with the horses to cut us off at the turn below."

## CHAPTER X.

### MORALIZING AND MUSIC.

The object of interest was a diminutive negro, clad somewhat in Eastern donkey-boy fashion; his one garment still more abbreviated by speed across fields. At the turn he caught the carriage, panting alongside as he offered trailing, thorny sprays, loaded with Cherokee roses and great bunches of creamy magnolia flowers, green tinted by reflected sunlight from their leaves. The Creole tossed him some small coin, and received the whole fragrant load; while the pickaninny rolled his great eyes and flashed teeth white as the magnolia petals in thanksgiving. Then he pulled the forelock of wool, braided with white cotton cord, and trotted back for fresh spoils.

"What a beauty! Such funny little bow legs! Oh! if they only grew so in the North!" Dalia exclaimed, her eyes, wandering from purchaser to vendor, causing rather mixed sequence of thought. "How happy they all seem down here," she added, coming back to logic, as was her wont.

"Yes, they are happy enough," Mrs. Winston replied to her last glance; "but were they a little less lazy and a trifle more clean, they might prove more useful to themselves and to us."

"But they will be some day, will they not?" the girl queried earnestly.

"Perhaps, at the—millennium," Latour answered.

"They are the happiest race on the face of the globe; but my experience of them, each time I return to this country, is that they grow worse and worse. The vices of slave days have descended. They imitate, but they do not really improve."

"Not by education?" the girl again asked. "Are not the schools bringing them into a higher life?"

"I certainly think they are," Mrs. Winston answered, decidedly. Stanch patriot! her pride forced defense of a Southern institution, though not of the South's making. "Why, General Latour, *our* negroes seem most anxious to learn; and there are many large enough to earn good pay, who sacrifice it to remain at school. Yes, Miss Dalia, I have great hope for the negro's future."

"*Peutetre*," the Creole answered, lazily. "But to me they always seem a larger growth of apes, with imitative and acquisitive traits more highly developed, and only lacking in the matter of tails. In India, Egypt, Louisiana, or Congress, I have found the black man at his best when—blacking boots!"

"I am afraid papa thinks a little as you do, Uncle Ad," Dalia replied thoughtfully. "But I really long to see them at their best."

"You shall!" he cried, decisively. "Perhaps we can not arrange a hen-roost in the dark of the moon for you, and baptism is hardly ripe thus early in the summer, but a picnic—they still have them, Mrs. Winston?"

"Daily, almost, in summer," the young matron replied; reminiscence smothering patriotism. "There is no length to which they will not toil and skimp, only to squander the last cent on the beloved 'Society!' And this is a charitable body—"

"There! I thought there must be good in them after all!" the Northern girl broke in, exulting.

"Which I do believe," Mrs. Winston quietly went on, "is organized chiefly to give its own picnics and attend those of its endless bands of brothers. They almost deprive us of servants during this festive season."

"Aping your Northern Anglomaniacs, Dalia," Latour laughed. "You see *their* season is in summer, like London's. But here we are at home!"

The carriage stopped at a hedge-bordered garden; the party alighted and, in the broad, gravelled walk, joined General and Mrs. Everett, Winston, Major Beaumont and Captain Rumford, who had preceded them, by carriage and horseback.

The wide, low galleries, completely surrounding the old, one-story house, were draped with vines and trailing moss; and the great windows of its high-pitched rooms overlooked the bay on one side, and on the other the far-spreading lines of tents. This house, volunteered by the owner, in Southern fashion as it stood, was to be the home of the Everetts, while guests of the city; and Winston, at the portal, said cordially but naturally:

"Your headquarters, Mrs. Everett. As General Latour's Eastern comrades might have said: 'This house and all it contains is yours!' Your *tent* is there, General"—he pointed to the great canvas under the old magnolias. "But we hope to make you feel that your *home* is here. I am not sure, Miss Dalia, that the piano is your favorite; but the Major chose it as the best in town."

Bennie Everett's lips moved tremulously, but no sound came from them, as she turned rather misty eyes toward the Gulf; and her hand again crept into that of the Southern wife at her side. Her husband—ever keeping his lover's intuition—came quickly to her rescue.

"I am afraid you are all trying to spoil my little secretary, Colonel," he said with genuine feeling. "But for us all, appreciation is too strong for words."

"And everything so perfect—so homelike, Dale!" his wife added, passing into the spacious old hall. "And did you ever see such loads of lovely flowers?"

Dalia was already at the piano, her eyes bright with pleasure, a happy smile showing pretty dimples in the flushed cheeks. She had tossed her sailor hat and gloves on the floor, and the strong, firm fingers were running over the keys with the certain clarity of the skilled pianist.

"You *are* too good, all of you," she said, naturally. "Papa is right; you will spoil me, and make me want to live among you in the South," and a sudden flush dyed the firm, fair throat and broad brow, as she glanced up.

Adrien Latour's eyes met hers; their gaze calm, steady and not intent, but with half-inquiry that was perhaps unmeant, certainly not understood. Next instant the nimble fingers flashed into the rhythm of a Chopin nocturne, artistically phrased and emphasized into true interpretation. The group, now inspecting other rooms, sent back a hum unheard by the player and equally by the Creole. He leaned over a chair-back, his lips in half-smile, his eyes following the hands that deftly pearled the piano. As they rested on the keys, the nocturne done, he said briefly:

" Play something different."

Half command, half entreaty as was the tone, the girl only answered by the massed harmonies of Rubenstein, handling the strong theme with easy power, well-mastered technique, and something beneath both that school may develop but can never make.

" She was right!" the man cried, impulsively. " Child, you are an artist!"

" *Who* was right?" Dalia ignored the compliment, but whirled the stool to turn wondering eyes upon the speaker. " What personal pronoun feminine has been discussing me, Uncle Ad?"

" Um!—what—eh?" Latour came back to himself with the disjected trio of exclamation. " I only meant, little girl, that your playing is remarkably good. You must let me hear you often this week."

" You love music, then?" she asked with interest.

" As an Indian loves red, from instinct, not reason," he answered simply. "I have heard the best, without understanding much of it, in many countries."

" But you *must* understand, if you feel it," the girl persisted. " No one can love Chopin, or Beethoven, who does not comprehend their soul, however little he may analyze the method. It is just like loving anything else; attraction, sympathy first, then pleasure, pain, devotion, which make their own understanding."

" A novel definition, and as novel as strong," the man said. He did not look at her, but again the soft surge of color swept her fair face, as she added abruptly:

" And equally absurd in a girl who has literally loved nothing else."

" I was not asking confessions or evasions," he retorted seriously. "All women must love something, be it the pug, the missionary meeting, or a man. No girl reaches her teens without finding her ideal doll and ripping down to his sawdust, more than once."

"You are mistaken!" Dalia was equally placid as emphatic now. "*I* never have had such a fancy, and I believe such a one would leave me poorer in maidenly feeling! What sensible girls can find in gawky boys, half educated, unread and usually stupid, has always puzzled me when I paused to think about it. For my own part, I have always preferred my music, a book, my horse, or, when I wanted a lark, to play tennis, climb trees and snowball with Spofford."

"The Captain Cushing of the staff?" he queried, as she paused to take breath.

"Yes; we've been great chums for years." She nodded brightly. "Having no brother and few congenial girl friends, I fear I grew rather boyish in my tastes; and Spofford was always ready to aid and abet. But *who* is 'she?'"

"Only one of your rare lady friends, who told me last night that you played well."

"Last night? why, I have no friends here," she answered, wondering.

"Is not Miss Moore in the list?" he asked with eyes full on her candid face.

"Miss Moore has always been quite nice to me; and I believe papa and mamma like her very well," Dalia answered simply. "But it would be absurd for a girl like me to call a woman of the world like her my friend." She paused, suddenly looking full in his eyes as she asked: "Do you like her?

"My dear child," the old soldier answered, "you will learn some day that most men always like pretty women, who—do not object."

The girl wheeled round on the stool; and the rattling brilliance of a waltz movement by Raff so promptly and completely harmonized with his thought, that Latour's mustache quivered in a smile, as he caught the *motif*. And it drew the others back to the parlor, where Winston asked for a song. Dalia sang, as interrupted musicians sing for those who break the current of tone-thought. But her German ballad was daintily colored, better phrased, and showed fair command of the queen-tongue of songs. Then Latour said, very quietly:

"You sing remarkably for a good pianist. Let us have your own favorite ballad?"

"I do not know that I have any," the girl answered, irresolute. "I do not pretend to sing. The piano is so much more reliable. It never gets 'out of voice.' But you know this?"

She played the prelude to Goring Thomas' fine song, "A Summer Night," singing the English words; rather carelessly at first, but warming with the theme into real power. The voice, a light contralto, of remarkable evenness and admirably managed, grew more sympathetic as the *motif* moved her; and the sustained low notes of the finale were rich and fruity with vibrant power, as she sang:

> "My heart was weary and oppressed
> With some sweet longing—half confessed!
> Ah! night of love! O! lovely night of June!
> Hast thou forgotten, love—so soon?"

"A beautiful song! Such admirable sentiment!" cried Captain Rumford, in perfunctory praise.

"The song is better than the sentiment," Dalia answered, bluntly. "There is too much 'ah! love' and 'my heart' in the translation. The English does no justice to Marzial's words."

"It rarely does to French or German songs," Latour answered. "And this, a great favorite of mine ever, is not a translation but a paraphrase."

"Give us something English then," asked the regular officer, perhaps more patriotic than critical. "You know some National airs?"

The girl glanced at him, half-amused; her eyes catching Latour's but an instant, as they fell on the keys again. Then she played, half-mechanically, the "Marseillaise," running it into the "Wacht am Rhein."

"These are the only two worth playing," she said, stopping abruptly. But her fingers softly stole over the keys in the refrain—

"Hast thou forgotten, love—so soon?"

Suddenly she caught herself with a start and half-blush; rising from the stool abruptly, as she said:

"Isn't it strange, Uncle Ad, that no English speaking people have a national music. 'God save the King' is a ponderous musical prig; and 'The Star Spangled Banner' is only a trifle higher than 'Dixie!'"

"Doubly treasonous speech, here!" her father cried. "I shall go over and assume command under the combined notes of both airs! Come, gentlemen; we name the camp at dress parade."

## CHAPTER XI.

### RIBBONS AND ROMANCE.

How rapidly days glide by, under even the dullest of military routine, all know who have followed the drum. Here, under the soft skies and moss-draped trees of a new land to them, the Everetts found that pleasant efforts of new friends added wings to the fleeting hours. The courtesies of strangers, that had greeted their arrival, soon mellowed into the easier attentions of intimates; and scarce any hour of the day found the cottage empty of visitors from town, largely reinforced by the braided and gilded youth from camp. Especially with the excited groups of pretty young Sponsors and Maids of Honor, Dalia had grown to be prime favorite; and "Camp Everett," as the cottage soon came to be called, was haunted by them and their brass-buttoned young beaux at not always convenient hours, en route to the grand stand, decorated with their colors on competition days, or to the lunches at the tents of "their boys." And great were the joys, proportionate was the woe, when those boys won, or lost, the longed-for prizes, with attendant chances for attachment of the long blue streamers to their chosen flags.

The Northern girl often sat among them, watching the soldierly bearing and admirable drill of the young competitors, with heightened color and dancing eyes; but only the blue-and-gray badge adorned her close-fitting and simple costume, that best advantaged her

6

lithe and graceful figure. But she gently refused all importunity to assume the sponsorship of one or another corps. To the first proffer, gracefully made by the captain of the champion drill team of the South, she had answered simply:

"I prize the compliment, Captain Morey, equally as I do the spirit that prompts it; but, as a stranger, I feel that some of these dear girls, who belong to you, should fill the place."

"It is our Southern pride to consider the sisters of our brothers-in-arms our own," the gallant soldier had answered, but Dalia had only shaken her head and persisted—

"That is just as nice as can be, but I am only a practical Yankee girl, and really do not comprehend the real meaning of it all."

"It is a custom at our Southern prize drills," the officer demurred, "and I think it rather a pretty one."

"Pretty, certainly; but is there any necessity for it?" the girl contended, in her insistent way of going to the bottom of all subjects. "Is there any real military good in it?"

"Not one bit in the world, Miss Everett," bluntly answered the young captain of B company; a character in his way, and quite as strong-willed as the girl. "It is one of those habits, like cigarettes and gossip, that fellows get into from pure imitation, and then can not break themselves of; but it is equally as unnecessary, though our boys think they can't live without them."

"Yet you have the belle of Mobile for B company's sponsor, Captain," Morey turned on him with the clincher.

"Force of bad example, purely," the other retorted. "Go on; tell Miss Everett that we are the junior company of the First; that I was private in your rear rank a year ago, and yet 'Sponse'—that's Bessie Brooke, Miss Everett—flaunts more ribbon for B than the Old Guard ever got from Napoleon. That's all true; and being so, it means nothing more military than the ices and cakes the girls send us, or the flirtations under tents inspired by them, plus our unmilitary champagne."

"It is a custom borrowed from chivalry," Captain Morey answered with dignity; "a reminder that every true knight chose his lady fair and fought for her to the death!"

"Saving your seniority," Captain Davitt retorted bluntly. "Those days were different from these; and those old fellows were go-as-you-please, catch-as-catch-can fighters, each for himself and all in happy ignorance of Upton's and fresh West Point judges!"

"You are right, Captain Davitt," Dalia chimed in merrily; "and, leaving out all poetry, to our modern eyes they were horrid prigs, very often. They were as grand heroes in simple blue or gray cloth as ever rode at Templestowe or Camelot! Why, papa or uncle Ad here was true a knight as 'godlike Arthur,' for all his Pendragon bonnet and steel vest! And as for Launcelot, *he* was more of the old beau and lady-killer than true knight, spite of his pondrous sword and 'wondrous horsemanship!'"

And Adrien Latour, catching the words, blew a great cloud and held his Havana suspended midway; and his black eyes saw the blue water line change to "Flirtation Walk," where a gauche cadet and a brilliant brunette girl moved out of the past and spoke the self-same words, now repeated under these far magnolias. What was there in this fair, frank, fresh-souled child, to ever wake old memories in him? What to ever stir anew long-sleeping phases of his nature, by sheer strength of congeniality.

But Dalia, falling back on filial piety, had shifted her burden to the plump shoulders of mamma, who assumed it with the gentle protest that "the child was not yet out; that the compliment was so conspicuous it might turn her head." And Latour, straight appealed to, came out out of his long travel into the past, with an absent-without-leave air, still sensibly averring his belief that:

"It would take more ribbon than all the camp possesses to turn that old head on such young shoulders! But Dalia appreciates the compliment the more, Captain Morey, coming from a corps as noted as yours."

"Indeed, I do, Captain! And so will papa," Dalia cried, warmly; adding with that irrepressible frankness of hers—"And, besides, I do not know if he would think it military. He is such a dear old martinet!"

"By which she means, Captain," Latour added drily, "that the General has a soldier's fondness for omitting from *ordinary* camps of instruction and school everything which does not add to efficiency and discipline."

So the ribbon streamers were bestowed elsewhere, and the Puritan's daughter clung to her bi-colored badge. And often at her side, spite of omnipresent button and frequent shoulder-strap, hovered the latest triumph of Robbie Pluffer's tailor, filling naturally, but not obtrusively, the post of looked-for and reliable walking-stick at need. And, alone with him, after the

custom of the town, but to the intense envy of braided
youth on duty, Dalia had explored the novel beauty of
"the old woods" below the shell road, and had praised
the high action of the spirited bay in the Pluffer dog-
cart. Moreover, she had retorted to Latour's rather
acid chaff in his own tongue, that the youth was far
from being the goose he adopted the air of being.

Miss Moore, too, had installed herself as chief of Mrs.
Everett's domestic staff, so she and Latour were constantly thrown together—"on duty," as she said—and
to him her manner was simply perfect; frank, friendly
and always pleasant, but never too gracious, or verging
toward the furthest boundary of sentiment. Together
they had gone as outriders to Dalia's expedition in the
Pluffer dog-cart, and the Creole's clear wit, and equally
clear eye, had failed to appreciate neither the woman's
rare powers as a talker, nor the perfect curves of a
figure that Worth had declared unsurpassed.

Homeward jogging, under dense shade of interlocked
trees, the subject of their talk drifted to art, Bella
Moore confessing that she did a little sometimes with
her brush.

"I could have sworn it," Latour answered promptly;
"something about you ever suggests inborn aptitude
for art."

The great brown eyes flashed quick query at his full-
turned face, but it was meaningless; the words were
but an accident of set speech, and the color mounting
to the rounded cheeks fell back. But she answered low
and slow:

"Some day, when we are better—older friends, perhaps, I may show you a trifle I am engaged on now. It

may surprise you, not as a work of art, but of—
memory."

Quicker than the brown eyes had sought his face, the
black now questioned hers, to find it placidly unconscious. Why, he could scarce have told himself, but a
vague, uneasy thought possessed him that the woman
meant more than the mere words she spoke. And again
and again that thought came back to him, through all her
bright talk of books, horses and people, until he lifted
her from saddle at the cottage door. Then, as she
turned on the step, Bella Moore said quietly, and as
though ending a long sentence:

"She had a haunting face—that model!"

She was gone before he had framed reply or question,
and Dalia, springing from the cart, was patting the
arched neck of his black and saying:

"Remember, Uncle Ad, I am to ride 'Jo. Johnston'
at daylight, for Mrs. Smythe calls 'assembly' for Dog
river at eleven o'clock."

## CHAPTER XII.

### THE NEGRO'S NIGHT PAGEANT.

Dalia found Major Beaumont on the porch, reclined in a great straw chair; his eyes suspiciously closed. But the veteran was promptly awake; and with his old-school bow said:

"My carriage waits you, dear young lady. Your father, mother, the Winstons—in fact half the visiting soldiery in camp—have gone to town. To-night offers a truly novel sight; indeed, one not to be seen save in our own Gulf City."

"And you waited, Major? You are always so good!" the girl exclaimed. "What is the sight?"

"Our negro 'firemen's anniversary' they call it," the old gentleman answered. "But really it is not commemorative of anything; and the darkeys are not firemen."

"How odd! What is it like?" she asked curiously.

"Like 'nothing on the earth beneath;' but it fulfills my pledge," Latour answered, as he joined them. "The Major is your good fairy and will now show you 'the negro at his best.' While not a hen-roost seen darkly, a baptism, nor yet a picnic, this is the concentrated essence of all three!"

Miss Moore quickly reappeared, gracefully fresh in exquisite summer toilette; and soon the quartette had joined the headquarters party on the club gallery in town, where it was reinforced by many citizens, and more visiting strangers, all expectant for the spectacle promised them. And novel as beautiful it certainly was; not only in glowing effect and well ordered progress, but at least equally in its lesson of the true status of those darker-skinned denizens of this section, perhaps the most discussed of all who dwell and vote therein.

Sitting serenely by her bay of future-promised greatness, letting the goods the gods of geography, commerce and investment provide drop gently into her wide-spreading lap, Mobile combines quaintly the pretty tastes and cherished traditions of ancestry with the more progressive methods of a wide-awakened to-day. She has long been recognized as *doyen* of those Mystic Orders of the Creole cities, which equally delight and puzzle visitors from afar on Shrove Tuesdays. But beside her Carnival, climate and herital love for prettiness and for sociality give the Gulf citizens many out-door pleasures, for which her bay-shore, her summer gardens and improving parks offer temptation by summer day and summer night.

Years ago a saucy writer dubbed her "The Picnic City," so frequent and enjoyed were these outings of her social clubs and numberless societies. And, even then, the black element added no little to the passing bands and street-processions that preceded these events on almost every summer's day.

In older days, reaching far *post bellum*—before invention, the "steamer," and last improved water-supply systems did away with volunteer fire departments in the more progressive South—"Firemen's Day" was red-lettered in each year's calendar. It was the gala of engines, decorated with elaborate designs, allegorical or

poetic; of flower-laden throngs on street, balcony and
doorstep; of thousands of uniformed firemen, largely
drawn from the better class of citizenship.   Lavish of
expenditure, full of educated taste and friendly rivalry,
these companies showed day-pageants equally as attractive to many thousands as were the wider-known—and
possibly more brilliant—display of the Mystics at Carnival time.

 During the four years of war, all pageantry ceased;
but after the peace, a new and eager element in the Gulf
section vied with the older one for precedence, at least
in the number of its unique out-door pleasurings.   And
—mimetic by instinct as the Simian of the Indian palm-
groves—the negro grew most covetous of the flaring
red shirt, as he was by structure careless of the head-
ache-producing glazed hat.   So, while no real fire
company of blacks was ever organized for work, numbers of imitators sprang up for play.

 "You have never had negro firemen at all?" Dale
Everett asked, when the Major explained all this  to the
party on the club gallery.

 "Never of negroes proper," was the answer.   "There
was one venerable and much-respected company, called
'Creole, Number One;' but its members were all of that
unique French Quadroon race, commonly miscalled
'Creoles,' who never were slaves and who had prepon-
derance of white blood.   Indeed, many of them owned
slaves; and were ever useful and respected citizens."

 "Did they pay taxes and vote?" Dalia asked, with
her usual curiosity in things that interest few women.

 "They paid taxes on what they owned," Winston
replied.   "But under the laws they had no votes."

"Oh, Colonel! Was that fair?"

"My dear young lady," Major Beaumont interposed, "your question is not. Out of uniform, our Colonel dispenses the laws—as they now are. So, naturally, he is scarcely competent witness as to their justice."

"But why are these negroes allowed to claim that they are firemen, if they never have been?" she persisted.

"Another illogical sequence," Latour put in. "Possibly, because they now can vote; and because many of them do so, not only early, but often."

"But I should suppose they would make good firemen," General Everett suggested. "They are agile, strong and fond of excitement."

"They lack stamina, 'grit,' I think," the old Major answered. "And that is the basis of good firemen always. Prince, here, was noted in the old volunteer system. I belonged myself, in the day of 'silk-stocking and ruffle-shirt' departments."

"General," Winston asked abruptly, "do you find that the negro makes a good soldier?"

"From limited personal experience I should say, no," Everett answered frankly. "Even where not lazy and careless about drill, he has little pride in his corps or himself."

"But he is capital fuse for the nimble political bomb," Winston said quietly. "The West Point experiment proved a costly failure; and in the army white soldiers can not be forced into affiliation with black."

"And none of your officers accept commands, without at least tacit protest," Latour rejoined.

"All of that is largely true," the Northerner assented.

"But my main **objection** to black enlistments is a practical one. White men make better soldiers ; and when we pay the same, it is preferable to get the best."

"That situation is one of the least hereditaments of the political upheaval," the Creole said quietly. "To me, every negro in uniform is but a marching political document, franked by an extremist politician ! "

"There seem to be few extremists down there ! " Everett answered with a smile, pointing to the street.

Far as eye could reach the pavements and door-ways were crowded with much-mixed humanity, as on no other occasion save, perhaps, Mardi Gras. And now, the throngs showed even larger proportion of black, brown and yellow faces. Dressed in their "best Sunday's," with faces shining in happy expectancy, adults of all ages—even dangerously small children—carried bouquets of every shape and value; from the simple bunch of bright ribbon-grass and field flowers, to the daintiest nosegay yielded by the gardens or hot-houses of this American *Firenze*. Among the dresses, the ladies noted flagrant combinations of color, and peculiar unfitness of cut to figure, in many cases; but, in the main, there was enough of neatness and contented comfort to make the blacks peculiarly interesting study to the Northern visitors. And to the local eye, more interesting still were those frequent groups of strange soldiers, in the uniforms of fifteen different States; now seeking each available point for seeing a parade that would have equally a novel interest and a startling lesson.

The distant glow of lights, haloed above the houses, drew nearer; as did the blare of several brass bands, ambitious, but not always in accord.

"They are coming!" Mrs. Winston said. "I do hope you will not be disappointed."

And almost with her words the head of the negro's unique pageant wheeled from another street, into that one passing the club-house. First marched a platoon of police, then, headed by an indescribable and most gymnastic drum-major, a large and handsomely uniformed band, blowing as though for life, and making no bad music for marching.

"Why, Uncle Ad, they are playing 'The Bonnie Blue Flag,'" Dalia cried. "And there is 'Dixie!'"

"Why not, Miss Dalia?" the Major interposed. "Mr. Lincoln adopted that rebel foundling."

"Not on Luther's principle, that the Devil should not have all the good tunes," she laughed back. "But look, mamma. If there isn't Carter!"

With that easy, lazy seat natural to the Southern black, Colonel Winston's steward rode his favorite chestnut, heading the parade as grand marshal. Immaculate evening dress set off his fine figure; his only decoration a wide, flowing sash of red and white, crossing his breast like a field-marshal's. But the chestnut charger was a marvel of loving decoration, its mane broad-plaited with ribbons of white and red, the saddle covered with crimson shabrack, gold-fringed and starred, while the tail was looped in many-bowed white and red, that swept the ground with every curvet.

"But, Uncle Ad," Dalia suddenly exclaimed, "there is not one blue ribbon with the white and red."

"These are the firemen's colors in all lands, Miss Dalia," the Major quickly deprecated, with his usual tact.

"And it is the irony of accident, rather than of destiny, that they are the Confederate colors also," Latour added grimly.

As he spoke, Carter's eye caught the group upon the gallery, his shining silk hat was lifted and angled at the marching salute, as his ribboned baton signaled the drum-major. Instantly, the rebel-yelling notes of "Dixie" glided into the "Star-Spangled Banner," as the band marched on amid renewed cheers and applause.

And following came an endless-seeming line of men, marching steadily, with evident pride in the glances of admiration, or curiosity, shot at them from many thousand eyes. All were shirted in white or red, their breast-shield bearing huge numbers. Each gripped with one hand the gilded and ribboned rope attached to the engine, within which moved the borrowed "engine horses," gaily decked and led by proudest of jockey-clad grooms. And every man, lifting his neat straw hat in salute as he passed, carried at least one huge bouquet — for it was the month of flowers in the Gulf City — and male and female friends of " dem 'ar' boys " seemed to have " robbed the cradle and the grave " of the floral Rachel, leaving her no children more to pluck. Special favorites, as pompous officers, noted men on the ropes, and especially visitors from many a neighboring town, bore two, three, half a dozen bouquets, while glittering trumpets — made mute by bright-tinted gags in their broad mouths — seemed veritable horns of floral plenty.

So rolled by three separate " machines," each vari-hued in color, taste and richness. And, prancing about the long and glittering line, dashed the black-clad, be-sashed marshals, proud and perspiratory beyond description, but all well mounted and managing their horses with that easy mastery coming only from early habit.

First rolled into view a disused steamer, drawn by four satin-coated black steeds, with glittering trappings; their labors sinecured by hundreds of strong hands upon the guide-ropes. On its smoke-stack—throned on satin and gold that was lost in beds of rare flowers—posed a very fair and pretty " Creole" child, richly costumed as Aurora. Another, equally pretty and graceful as attendant nymph, reclined upon the driver's seat, transformed to a bank of bullioned satin, hidden almost under flowers.

" Why is this called 'Merchants, Number One, Major," Everett asked, as shining reflectors and glowing red-fire showed him the gold-lettered ribbons of baptism. " Are any of them business men?"

" Another victory for the illogical, I fear," the veteran answered. " Rather, I should say, of the imitative. Our old 'Merchants' company was once famous in fire, as in social, matters.

" And why is Aurora their patron?" Dalia queried with much interest. " Is it to typify the day breaking for their race?"

" Scarcely so deep a reason, my dear young lady," he answered with a smile. " We have learned now to accept the pretty facts of negro pageantry, without delving for their derivation. Possibly Aurora is posing as the goddess of flowers for the nonce."

" How funny!" the girl laughed; suddenly growing grave, as she added: " But it does seem a pity that so much natural taste and beauty-love should not have direction, from care and education—Oh! Colonel, look at Dunkie!"

Forth rode Winston's chief groom, as chief-marshal of "Protector, Eleven," with all the grave rigidity of "The Cid," statued. in polished jet. From shining beaver to patent-leather pumps, no touch of color showed on man or horse, save white-shirt front, white eyeballs and white, gleaming teeth. For the negro was in full evening dress, *de rigeuer*, and his jetty steed bore only the tail ribbons to match his sash.

Behind its chosen band, the old-fashioned hand-brake engine rolled into view; transformed into a towering, rocky peak. Upon this rested a bright, golden eagle, its huge wings outspread. And from its beak floated broad ribbons, respectively legended in gold: "*Ferat qui Meruit Palmam!*" and "*Prior Tempore, Prior Jure.*"*

Dalia's quick eye caught the mottoes; and she turned to Mrs. Winston in triumph, as she cried:

"There! I knew Uncle Ad was teasing me, when he said the negro never improved. They have Latin devices for their clubs!"

"Which no one of them understands, I fear," Mrs. Winston deprecated. "But this really was the first of the negro imitators; so the ribbon tells truth."

"As it is too frequently told, by accident," the Major added. "I fear the picnic, not the schoolmaster, was abroad when this company swelled to such proportions as to necessitate that."

He pointed to the on-coming crowds of "Protector,

---

* Description of these decorations are not fanciful, but are accurately detailed from those of a recent pageant of these supposititious firemen, in Mobile streets.—THE AUTHOR.

Twelve;" pageant-born offspring of the passing company that vied with it, both in numbers and in bouquets.

Behind each engine, too, rolled showy four-in-hands and handsome open carriages; their liveried drivers feeling all importance of the occasion and showing gleaming ivories at every cheer. These vehicles bore the officers and honoraries of the companies, as well as hosts of invited brethren from many a neighboring town, hospitably called to share the glories of the march. All the occupants were immaculate in evening dress, and many almost buried under floral offerings of friends. Some of these were hurled, as the victims passed, by hands more loyal than discreet. For Dalia saw one wizened, white-haired negro almost covered by flowers piled upon his seat. Suddenly, as she looked, a ponderous mass of bright flowers hurtled through the rose-lit air, and, simultaneously, the aged black doubled up like a jack-knife, with hideous grimace of pain. There was dead silence in the throng about him, until a woman's voice crashed through it with the cry:

"Bress de Lor'! Da fool nigger dun hit de pasture in de win'!"

Headed by more marshals and another good band, "American, Numb Fourteen," closed the richly colored pageant. It was drawn by four splendid grays, led by handsome jockeys; the trappings of man and horse sparing noth' of costly glitter. And with it marched more l. of white-shirted and helmetted men, bearing on the gilded ropes. And this truck was one huge mound of rare and glowing flowers; upon them resting the gilded antlers of "championship," surrounded by four gleaming silver fire-buckets, to speak its plethora of treasury.

So the novel pageant passed, an ever-shifting kaleidoscope of color from flowers, uniforms and decorations, lighted by hundreds of reflectors and tinted into almost fairyland, by lavish use of colored fires. And all along its lengthy route of march plaudits and applause rang out, equally from the whites as from the blacks, though the enthusiasm of the latter mounted almost to camp-meeting temperature.

But no faces among the many thousands on the densely-packed streets of the old city that night showed such earnest interest, such wondering surprise, as those of the Northern visitors, who had been told such fairy tales of Southern life, but such very different ones from those realities they saw!

As the officers lit their cigars on the cottage porch, an hour later, Everett said gravely :

"I have studied the status of the Southern blacks somewhat, Major, but to-night has been a revelation to me. And you really mean that these men—these thousands so cheered and so brilliant—are not real firemen?"

"No one of those youngsters has ever been on a 'machine,' probably never at a fire, save to look on," the Major answered. "It is pure imit 'on. They borrow engines, horses, ideas probably. They save all the year and pay up dues, with eye single to this gala night."

"And the recurrent picnics," Latour added. "But, Dale, it shows the negro has so⸴⸴⸴⸴ ⸴o."

"It shows more," the Northerner answered quietly. "It proves, beyond dispute, that if the negro, in a typical Southern city, can thus display his pleasure-love on his own easily-won money, there must be little more than words in all extremist-prate about hand-cuffs, poverty and intimidation."

7

## CHAPTER XIII.

### IN WILLFUL WOMAN'S WAY.

Clear, sharp ring of the bugle sounded through the camp, returning in soft echo from surrounding woods; the broad flag of the Union climbed lazily after the lanyard to the peak of its tall peeled pine, then flapped out to display its thirty-six stars proudly to the Southern breeze. Hum of voices rose from the company streets, as half-waked men tumbled out of tents, tugging at refractory buttons, as they fell in for roll-call; cooks scurried from the wood-piles with fuel for mess-fires; and yawning negroes, lazily stretching gaunt limbs, shuffled to the great, pine-planked mess halls, "gitt'n' reddy fur brekfus.'"

There was delicious coolness in the dawn air, just touched with salty dampness; and dew hung beaded on leaf and weed, emphasizing the wood-scents still heavy in it, before the coming sun changed each drop to diamond and bade it disappear.

Somnus was still regnant god about "Camp Everett" cottage, three hundred yards away; itself seeming to sleep in embrace of great tree-arms—moss bearded and crowned with cream-cupped flowers—and caressed by clinging clasp of vines. But just as the pink glow above the flat Eastern Shore deepened into presage of sudden sunrise, Adrien Latour appeared on the gallery, booted and spurred for a ride. And just then, Colonel Winston's own groom trotted out from the cavalry stables, mounted on a slim, handsome chestnut and leading Jo. Johnston, with lady's saddle upon his glistening back.

The old cavalry leader pulled his long moustache absently, as he stepped to the gravel and scanned the approaching horses. For no lady had yet backed that massive black; no female hand had ever essayed control of that small, clean-muzzled head, with its human, wide-set eyes and keen-pricked ears, now tossing restlessly at every move of the cord-muscled neck.

"How's Jo. this morning, Dunkie?" he asked, as the negro slid backward from the chestnut and stood at the' black's head. "In good temper, eh?"

"Fo de lor,' boss, Jo. he hain't got *no* temper, 'scusin' he kind'er playful. He kinder fretful, too, dis' s'morn-in!'" And Dunkie showed glittering ivories and dodged the snap of the black's teeth, as Latour inspected the stirrup and girth and tightened the surcingle one hole. Then he moved round the horse, handling him gently, patting the restless neck; finally standing before him, when the lank muzzle stretched out and rested on his shoulder.

"Sho's yo born, boss," Dunkie chuckled, "da' hoss know you 'ready better'n me! 'Spec' yo done hoodoo Jo. enyway. Reck'n lak da' lady kin ride sum?"

"Oh, yes, Dunkie; she's a good rider," the white responded in fraternity of horse-talk; "she rides Miss Moore's bay better than her owner; and your boss says that no lady ever got so much out of the chestnut there. By the way, has the Colonel ever taken Jo. over big jumps? I've only tried him at logs and small ditches, but he takes them in his stride. Can he do stiff fences?"

"Yessah, boss! Jo. *kin* jump, I reck'n, wen he feel lak it," the groom answered with all his race's indirectness. "Wen'e want'er, Jo. kin jump over hisself; but sometime he refuse."

"He won't refuse this morning, unless I am much mistaken," Latour answered, confidently.

"Dun'no, boss," Dunkie scratched the head he shook wisely. "No lady ain't never rid 'im yit, an' hit's all sperament; fo' de Lor! hit *is !*"

As he spoke Dalia tiptoed from the door, in eager curiosity; a glass of milk in one hand, a goodly slice of bread in the other, and cheeks unduly plump in the double effort to masticate and talk.

"Isn't he just beautiful!" she cried, with a sudden freedom of speech. "Let's be off, Uncle Ad! But won't you have a milk-punch, as Major Beaumont would say, ' for a wakener ' ? "

"Rum before sunrise, Miss Everett? What an offer to a Frenchman! Now, if you had a nip of absinthe; but, as you have not, I'll run in and have a glass of milk. Seriously"—he paused in the doorway—"except in the field when rainy, I never took alcohol before breakfast in my life. Until that meal, I am as perfect a model as a gallant young captain, who promised ' her '— his mother, never to drink or smoke."

"You mean Spofford," the girl said simply, with her mouth full; adding earnestly: "He promised me, not her. You know, Uncle Ad, Mr. Cushing had a little weakness for wine; and that troubled his wife so much that I begged Spofford, years ago, never to drink or smoke, and—he never will! "

Latour's black eyes were fixed, with earnest scrutiny,

upon the clear, calm face of the girl; unconscious of it as she buttoned her gauntlet. Then he stepped to the black's side, holding his hand out for her foot, as he said: "I change my mind about the milk; as I do—about bread and butter—sometimes."

Jo. Johnston looked around curiously at the unusual pose of his accustomed rider, but he stood as still as a black statue, until Dalia was mounted, her skirt and stirrup arranged, and Latour stepped off to spring on the chestnut. Then, with a fierce snort and sudden shake of the head, the black snapped at the bit and reared straight in the air, ready for a bolt as he came down. But he miscalculated the firm, ready hand that wrenched the bit sideways as he rose, loosened the head full out, only to hold it powerless as the clean forelegs landed again with a jolting plunge. Another snort, another vicious shake at the taut bit, and again the black reared straight in the air.

"Stand away from his head!" The girl's voice rang out clear and sharp, the ring of command in it dropping Dunkie's uplifted arm and re-assuring Latour, as he stood tense and expectant, ready to grasp the rein if need came. But it did not. Quick loosing the bit as the horse rose, Dalia brought the whip down on his head in two rapid strokes; the next moment checking his descent so sharply that he recoiled almost on his haunches, but recovered and stood still and quiet, at the strongly emphasized "Whoa!"

A moment more, she had reached over patting his neck, Latour had mounted and the pair cantered off to the dirt road, followed by the negro's:

"Fo' de Lor'! Mars' Latter right. Da gal *kin* ride!"

"I did not want to whip him," Dalia said, with a mournful little smile, as her escort drew alongside, "but I could not have a circus right there on the gravel, wake mamma and be ordered to change horses. I think he knows me now. Does he often try to bolt that way?"

Latour gazed on the bright face, freshened by morning air, the slim, firm contours of the plain habit and Miss Moore's words, "on horseback an Amazon," sounded in his ears. But he only said quietly:

"There are some things you understand pretty well, Dalia, horses and music, for example. No, he does not bolt, but the first touch of the skirt is a ticklish novelty."

They rounded the camp, passed the sandy, odor-laden lanes and rode around the old Magnolia race course, famous in turf annals from its ownership by genial Captain "Bill" Cottrill, and the great horses he sent thence; equally famous in social memory from the old-time meetings when blood and beauty—human and equine—had illustrated brilliant days lang-syne. Then the soldier pointed out the rotting piers of that long wharf, at which the Federal army disembarked, thence marching up the Shell road to occupy Mobile; and thence striking through the pine woods, they struck sand road once more.

"This is the Dog river road," the man said. "You will hear its beauties from Robbie, later. But there is a flower-garden for the practical!"

He pointed to great spreading fields of green, low and tremulous in the now fresh breeze as the bay behind them; a veritable ocean of cabbages. Closer to them, skirted by a bridle path leading from the road, rows of seemingly endless forcing-shades flashed back the slant

rays of the sun in glances of fire ; no fence being neces-
sary along their line, as cattle and predatory prowler
would alike respect the brittle, shining barrier.  But
cantering past these, they struck the road once more;
where a  high, strong rail fence prevented unbidden entrance.

Jo. Johnston was now bowling along at easy gallop ;
well warmed up, but obedient to lightest touch of the
hand he recognized as that of a mistress.  A narrow
bridge spanned a gully water-shed ; and Latour, giving
the girl the planks, took the jump as matter-of-course in
the chestnut's stride.

" That was a little one ! " Dalia laughed.  " This fellow must jump splendidly.  Did you ever try him, Uncle Ad ? "

" Only over fallen trees and gullies," he answered.
" He is built for a jumper; but there seem few places to
test him in my rides."

She did not reply and they skirted the great field,
until it narrowed to a mere strip; the tall fence on
the north, the glinting panes of the long-ranged hot-
houses on the south.  Before them, a mile northward,
gleamed the white of the tents ; and sight of them
caused the girl to cry :

" So near home !  What a short ride !  Oh !  Uncle
Ad, I must have one jump before we go in."

" Not on that level stretch ahead," he answered, with
a smile.  But it faded quickly, as the girl suddenly
wheeled her horse and cantered over the plateau toward
the fence just left behind.  He was beside her in a moment, saying:

" Dalia !  You are not mad enough to try that fence."

" I've taken a higher one," she answered.

" Yes; on your own horse; on ground you knew. The landing in that field is plowed and soft — perhaps ditched. The bare thought is folly ! "

"Are all men always wise, that they expect women to be so ever?" the girl asked, coldly ; and, now thirty yards from the fence, she tightened her hold on the reins and, with quick motion, swept her skirt beneath the stirrup foot. Latour, his face set in hard, angry anxiety, touched the spur and rode past her, as he cried :

" Check him !  You shall not ! "

"Papa says that to me—*rarely!* " was the clear retort, without one glance; for her eyes were fixed on the top rail, though a light, not wholly of excitement, glittered in them, as she braced herself and touched the horse with her switch.

" *Becassine !* " muttered the Creole through set teeth, as he cast loose stirrups and prepared to vault to ground. But the teeth opened into a smile as the black answered the whip by tossing head and a flirt into air of his heels. And he called :

" Steady, Dalia !  Look out, he will refuse ! " just as the horse swerved and declined to try the ugly jump. But, with a toss of her own head and a sharp cut across his, Dalia cantered him straight back over the level, turned him, and again put him at the fence.

Her face was pale, no dimples in the cheeks now ; the close-pressed lips full of determined temper and the eyes—steadily fixed on the top-rail —glinting with anger. And Latour's face, too, was stern-set and darker than its wont, as he sprang from saddle and grasped the black's bit with one motion; calling sharply :

"Whoa! boy—steady!"

With a jolting break in his stride, the black stood still, obedient to strong will and strong arm; the girl sitting firm in saddle; her cold, gray eyes firmly meeting the angry black ones.

"Dalia, this is madness!" he exclaimed.

"Perhaps worse," she retorted, with a tone hardened by anger. "It might be called—rudeness!"

"But the danger, child "—

"You should not have ridden with a—child!" she cried; a great surge of color dyeing brow, cheek and neck. And tightening her reins the girl raised the whip in her right hand, as she added imperatively:

"Please let go my rein, General Latour!"

For one instant the blood tingled in Latour's cheek, for he doubted whether the switch was raised for him or for the horse. The next, his face softened, as did the voice that answered:

"I have never disobeyed a lady's imperative command, Dalia. But your father—your mother—are my dearest friends; almost my only ones. In face of certain danger, I do for their child what Dale Everett had done in my place. So much to my comrade's daughter. Now, I obey the lady's command."

There was no emphasis on any word; no tone of anger, reproach; none even of excuse, in the speech. Nor was there undue haste in the movement that, at once, released the horse's head and placed him again in saddle at her side.

The angry blood fell out of the girl's face, leaving it deadly pale; but she turned her horse so that he could not see her eyes, shook the bit and sent him bounding

campwards.     Not one word was spoken as they sped
around the camp, through the scented woods and up the
cottage drive; none until Latour, springing from saddle
at the door, lifted the girl to the gravel path.

Then she turned her face full to his; calm, resolute,
with the candid eyes looking steadily into his own. And
the voice was low, musical, but without one tremor of
struggle, or of conquest, that said:

"I *am* a child, a silly, spoiled and self-willed one.   If
you can not forget my rudeness, my ingratitude, please
try to forgive it.   You are the first to show me myself.
I shall not forget the lesson, and, General Latour, I
thank you for it."

Still looking full in the soldier's eyes, and still with
her clear-cut face, calm and pale, Dalia Everett slipped
off her gauntlet and extended her firm right hand.

And her father's comrade—without one word of answer, with no lightest touch of courtiership, but with
the deference he had shown to a queen dethroned—bent
his tall head and touched that hand lightly with his lips.

## CHAPTER XIV.

### A RIDE TO A FINISH!

The picnic at Dog River proved a great success. Mrs. Winston had taken Mrs. Everett—now her fast friend—Major Beaumont and Colonel Clarke, the Ohian, in an easy-riding carriage; Mrs. Smythe and her *caro sposo* with Captain Rumford and Bella Moore were the horseback party; while Dalia was escorted by the attentive Robbie Pluffer and Bessie Brooke by Captain Cushing who was now markedly devoted to the pretty sponsor.

Early that morning the Governor of the State had telegraphed Colonel Winston of his arrival at noon, to hold review and inspection the succeeding day; and, as Latour and his Excellency had been army comrades, General Everett had assigned the former to command of the cavalry escort of reception. And, as the horses were led off from the cottage, after his ride, the Creole had received the formal and red-lined order of assignment from the hands of Captain Cushing. Whether with, or without, deep sorrow Latour had penned a note full of it to Miss Moore, and another to Captain Rumford, who was fortunately off duty for the day; had donned uniform and sabre for the first time and clattered up the Shell road at head of two hundred sabres, to meet the State Commander-in-chief.

And Bella Moore, like the wise virgin she was, accepted with seeming thanks the goods the gods provided; and Latour's excuse of "sudden detail on duty,"

at the same time. If any disappointment lurked under
the olive braided bosom of her tailor-made habit, the
gallant regular by her side never suspected it, from
her brilliant wit and joyous deportment "all the long
day."

The weather was perfect; fleecy clouds considerately
veiling the sun from too close prying into female com-
plexions; and, likewise aiding the catch of the fishers of
the party. These had boated out to the fishing grounds,
scarce ruffled by the gentle south wind; and the others
had poled about through grass and water-lilies nearer
shore; or wandered under the forest giants, bending
Narcissus-like above the stream and nodding grave
approval of reflected grandeur.

Later lunch had been served from the hampers of the
ambulance, reinforced by their own catch. The beer
was found to be ice cold; and the Major had put the
claret in the sun.

"It is a barbarism of the young generation," he had
informed Colonel Clarke, "to cool good claret. Ice is
only useful, sir, to hide demerits of inferior wine, by
freezing the palate out of power to detect a high grade.
This wine, laying on the ice in the ambulance, needs the
sun for an hour to regenerate it. Your good claret is
the Parsee of light wines."

Then that veteran of the old school, inconsistent, as
most zealots are, had brewed his peculiar "claret-cup"
with mint and cordials and lemon; icing it to near
freezing point and loosening all tongues by its cunning
secrets.

Coming down to the river, Robbie Pluffer's party had
ridden in a light and somewhat cramped surrey, with

stationary canopy-top, held by iron uprights. His team
was scarcely a matched one, being his own banged bay
and a restive, hard-mouthed sorrel, once used by Mr.
Smythe as a roadster, but later relegated for bad behav-
ior to farm service. But Robbie was a careful if not a
brilliant whip; and the down trip had been made with
no result more alarming than hard bumping over frequent roots and crazy bridges of the old woods road.
But, with natural courtesy, perhaps warmed by the
Major's claret-cup, the Mobilian had proffered the box-
seat, homeward bound, to Captain Cushing and the
blonde maiden of the ribbons. And, whether this
renunciation was born, in part, of Mr. Pluffer's desire
for a cosy, back-seat *tete-a-tete* with her, Dalia never
knew. But, informed of it, she had only remarked
drily :

"I had supposed Spofford, as a staff officer, was more
a rider than a driver."

And now, the party, marshaled at the fisherman's
house by Mrs. Smythe, was gay with reminiscent pleasures of the day; the ladies, crowned with festoons of
gray old moss and bearing huge bunches of delicate wild
flowers. The horseback party were mounting, the two
girls were in the surrey and the elders were looking
over the water at the fast-graying sunset. Suddenly,
and before Cushing had well-grasped the reins, the big
sorrel, snorting and plunging, tore his bit from the little
negro at his head; making a half-turn and bolting for
the bank. But, by quickness and presence of mind,
Captain Rumford caught the dragging rein, twisted the
brute's ugly head and held him till the negroes caught
the bits and the lines were secure in Cushing's hands.

Then, slightly flushed, but dignified as ever, the latter turned and said:

"I hope you were not alarmed, ladies."

"Not in the least," Dalia answered quietly; but adding, as she looked straight at the sorrel's ears, "this time!"

"Oh! have you stopped them?" cried the little sponsor, with eyes tight shut and little hands tight pressed over her ears. "And I thought, Captain Cushing, you were such a brilliant driver!"

"Brilliant drivers are plentiful," Dalia said, quietly. "There is only one good driver; the careful one."

Robbie Pluffer, had propriety permitted, could have hugged the Yankee girl for the speech; while the Yankee boy, choking down retort, took the limber whip from the socket and dropped it on the sorrel, cause of his reproof.

"I wouldn't whip them, I think," Dalia said once more; as the dash the brute gave jolted them roughly over the root-lined road, before the strong arms of the youth reduced them to a steady trot again. "That off-horse is fretting enough now; and he'll pull you out if you do not quiet him."

The young soldier sat silent, but sulking the more as his box neighbor's musical laugh rang through the woods:

"Dear me, Dalia! *What* a girl you are! I do believe you could drive as well as Captain Cushing!"

"Possibly," Miss Everett answered quietly. "I have never seen him tested yet." ·

\* \* \* \* \* \*

While Major Beaumont was brewing his claret-cup at

Dog river, Adrien Latour had slipped away from the headquarters tent, bored by the rather too effusive welcome to Southern soil of his Excellency, the Governor, to his Union comrade. He lounged absently over to the now deserted cottage, and—his uniform coat changed for riding-jacket—stretched full length on a settee, his head resting on hands clasped behind it.

Under the fervid Egyptian noon of twenty years ago, he had thrown himself on his divan, in just such a mood and just such pose. And the eyes that had then gazed out unnoting the desert's sea of sand, now took as little cognizance of broad blue bay and bellying sails of yachts and saucy little tugs compelling great hulls of timber-ships. Those wide-open eyes were turned inward, and through memory's mirage rose the old homestead parlor by the Hudson, where youth's angry pride had lied to its first love; dissolving away to be replaced by a dim chamber in Cairo, where another woman—white-draped, pallid, remorse-stricken, had told that his newer love was but a living lie; this picture quick replaced by the fresher one of that morning, where the daughter of that early love had defied him—yielded and prayed grandly for forgiveness.

Whether following his day-dream, or from restlessness alone, the Creole could not himself have told, but he rose suddenly, tossed away his cigar, and strode rapidly toward the cavalry stables, just as the bugle sounded assembly for evening dress-parade.

Ten minutes later he was cantering Jo. Johnston toward that level stretch bounding the cabbage-field of the morning's episode. And, as he rode, quick changes swept the man's face; now lighting into a smile, half-gratified, half-amused; again clouding under some memory that compressed lips and knotted brow.

"What a child!" he muttered, as he entered the straight stretch facing the fence. "A spoiled one, too; but more her father's daughter than her mother's! *Um!* had the chestnut been able to carry me over, I believe I'd have let her try that fence!"

His eye rested on the tough top rail of the zig-zag, strong barrier; and the smile again played about his eyes, as he leaned over and stroked the black's great neck

"Now, *we* will try it, boy, and see whether I was right or wrong!"

Lightly shifting the reins, he turned the horse's head to the fence, carrying him to the jump at full gallop. Evenly Jo. Johnson went to it; but, four yards away, he switched his tail, balked, and again refused.

"Obstinate, too, and high-strung!" Latour muttered. But he still smiled as he walked the black to the rails and held him there, patting his neck before he turned and cantered back. Rather sullenly shaking his head, the black made another rush dead at the fence; but, four feet away from it, swerved sharply to the right, with swing that had shot a worse rider from saddle like stone from sling. But the strong left hand jerked the restive head back so to the rail and almost nosing it.

For an instant the black hesitated, quivering; gathered, as if to take the jump standing; then, with sudden snort and three fierce kicks, began bucking with agility that shook even the firm-seated rider nearly from his saddle.

Both smile and flush were on the Creole's face now,

from exercise, or something else, as he sent the spurs home at every jump; still muttering with every gaff:

"So, I *was* right, Master Jo.! A nice lady's horse, you! Lucky I insisted!"

Then he loosed the black's head, letting him bolt at will, in vain effort to escape the pricking spur—inexorable as "the black rider" on the pillion of classic poem. At last the horse was held up, still and panting, on the very spot whence he had thrice been sent at the jump. Springing to ground his rider scrutinized girth, bits and breathing; moving round the horse with quiet words and firm touch, as the great sides gradually settled to regular heave. Then, stroking the lean muzzle, he said, as though to human friend:

"Now, old boy, we will get over that rail, or carry it with us."

He was in saddle again; the reins steadied, then lightly shaken loose. Without word, or touch, the black threw out his head, went at the fence in full run and, never pausing for spring, cleared rail and blind ditch beyond, in a flying leap! So strong was his rush, that his great stride crashed through plowed land and cabbages, half across the narrow strip of field, ere Latour raised his eyes toward the low, glassed sheds, gleaming dangerous beyond. Then the caught a sight that made his blood creep cold, even with his trained presence of mind took it in at one glance and drove both spurs cruelly home.

*   *   *   *   *

Captain Cushing's team was going steadily, but under heavy enough pull to flatten the boy's broad back and keep his elbows straight, when Dalia had replied to

Bessie Brooke. The driver could not turn round, but retorted over his shoulder :

" Perhaps you would like to try this team, Miss Dalia? I'll resign if——"

The sentence was never finished. They were at the broad turn from the old woods into the cart trail ; sandy and heavy, but narrow, when Bella Moore dashed by at full gallop, leading the other riders a hundred yards. Her skirt flapped close to the big sorrel. Into the air he went with a vicious snort, rearing nearly straight; his ugly head shaking the bit loose, to clamp it in his teeth as he came down and bolted for the road.

Cool, steady, but a trifle pale, Cushing bore on the left rein; guiding the quieter horse into the roadway, as his crazed mate dragged him on in full run. Then the boy leaned over, looped the lines about his hands and braced himself for desperate pull as he called, through clinched teeth :

"Hold on, Miss Brooke! Hold tight, Miss Dali ' Keep cool; there's no danger!" And he gave a gre.. sway on the lines, that had such effect on the now racing team, as it might have had upon a wild locomotive.

Bessie Brooke obeyed half of his behest. With open mouth and eyes tight closed, she did hold on ; one little hand gripping the iron standard of the surrey's top, the other his tense left arm.

Robbie, to his credit, braced himself as best he might, on the cramped back seat; half-turned to Dalia, to steady her at need, in that terrible jolting over roots and ruts. And the girl, grasping a standard rod firmly with one hand and the seat's back with the other, showed him a face as unmoved, though pale, as had the wild team been only in a trot.

" Is the road ahead straight ? " she asked Pluffer.

" For two miles ; then comes a ——." A fierce jolt cut off the answer and his breath, at once ; but the girl, braced by her arms, again asked quietly :

"Any bridges ? "

" Three—beyond the curve—bad ones ! " The reply was shaken out of him in sections.

"Don't brace yourself so stiff; swing with the jolts ! " Dalia answered, briefly, as though on parade. "Are we likely to meet any teams coming down ? "

" Not so late as this," he answered more easily, following her advice.

" That's lucky," she said, half to herself. "Are they pulling you out, Spofford ? "

" No ; I can hold 'em ! " the boy answered, bravely ; adding with a half-gasp, as the brutes made a fresh lunge from a white stump : " Hold on, Miss Brooke ! "

Dalia was silent, but her eyes ran carefully over the cramped seats, high back and low roof of the surrey ; slender uprights bending with every jolt—slight wheels humming like tops.

Suddenly she half-turned, the thud of pursuing hoofs striking her ear.

" She's gaining on us—Miss Moore ! " she whispered to Robbie. " But she is alone ! "

Bella Moore's thoroughbred had pulled further away from her companions and now, spite of their mad rush, was gaining on the runaways. They heard, too ; pursuit adding fresh fright to their crazed brains.

On they speed ! On, over root and log and stone ; on,

down the slope to the black creek, to the frail swaying bridge; upon it; over it, the flying cart rocking till relieved wheels spin round in air, on one side then the other.

On, too, presses the pursuing rider, her clear voice shouting:

"Hold tight, girls! The road ahead is clear! Don't jump!"

Rattle, crash, thud of hoofs alone break stillness of sunset woods. No word is spoken for a quarter mile, but two red discs in Cushing's cheeks suddenly drop out of them, his breath coming in quick, short gasps.

Deadly pale, striving to brace himself afresh, the brutes jerk him half-around, nearly from the seat, as his left arm yields. Relieved of pull on that side, they swerve from the road into that very tree-strewn path Dalia had passed at dawn.

With new speed from lessened pull, on straight to the open garden plot—straight to the deadly pits, low-sashed with glass! the mad brutes fly, their great plunges racking the surrey fiercely. Then a grinding crash against a tree; spokes, tire, hub whirl in air and the wagon, lurching to right, falls over on its side.

Bessie Brooke hurls from her seat, striking Cushing and rolling to the sand, throwing him against the iron upright, which pins him down where he falls. Robbie rolls from the back seat like a ball! but Dalia—thrown against him—falls back and catches in the surrey's top!

On dashes the mad team, tearing the broken cart through heavy sand and snapping undergrowth!—On, straight for the lined glass eyes, that flash back the level rays of sunset! But over thud of hoof and crunch of limb Cushing hears that low rich voice he loves—now with the agony of pleading in it, moan out:

"Don't *pull!* Oh! *don't* pull!"

Powerless from the weight upon him; bruised and faint from shock and pain; cruelly dragged along, with every spurn of four iron heels hurling dirt into his face —almost grazing his hair!—the boy hears her moan crash through danger, peril and pain into his very soul. He can not turn his head, but lightning-swift thought pictures that one woman of all women to him, bruised, mangled—dying, perhaps; that plaint wrung from the soul he knows so brave, by agony of her imagined tearing from the wreck. Helpless, agonized—the reins still wrapped round his extended hands—he lies an instant that seems an age; and could man's hair whiten in a moment of supreme horror, his had turned silver then!

But, almost with the girl's voice, came another, strong, cheery, vibrant:

"Up, boy! over! *Whoa!*"

And with that voice, crash and clink of glass—shock and shivering jar—then dead stop; and Spofford Cushing loses all in darkness.

Midway in the narrow garden strip, Latour sees the surrey dragging straight for the deadly sashes. With no pause for thought—quicker than thought itself— both spurs drive home. The grand black, spurning plant and furrow, nears the wide glasses; is lifted at them with voice and hand and heel.

His great jump falls short; man and horse crash down, sending up flare of splintered wood and glass!

But now they are out, facing the thundering team; again the spur, the loud, vibrant *Whoa!*—and the great black shoulders strike the sorrel full in the side, rolling him under the bay who plunges once, then comes to his knees!

Ere the black recovers from the fierce recoil that brings him to his haunches, Latour springs from saddle; lifts the pale, dust-covered girl from the wreck—with one quick-satisfied glance of inquiry—then obeys her mute command to raise the surrey from the crushed boy beneath!

## CHAPTER XV.

### THAT NIGHT OF JUNE.

Bella Moore strolled slowly up the long pier, her hands softly clasped before her, for Adrien Latour's arm was busied with unaccustomed care of a stout cane, reminiscence of his late escapade.

It was the last night of the week, and of the encampment as well. Already many scattered commands had struck tents and dispersed homeward ; those who bore away the blue streamers of victory followed by cordial cheers of the vanquished in this peaceful contest of arms. Sponsors and maids were somewhat desolated at prospect of speedy relegation to mere black-coated beaudom ; and who may tell but that more than one little heart beat quick " tattoo "—but mournful, past tears—when its special capture waved his cap in farewell, as he sped to other fields of victory, or conquest ? Now only Winston's local regiment and the Northwestern Brigade held the half-deserted village of canvas; and at early morn Everett, with all his family and following, would take train for home, at the railroad crossing near.

Miss Moore was saying her last words in her last walk with the Creole, and her tone was low but earnest.

"But I insist it *was* heroic, General ! As I rode up, at safe distance, I could see—yes, and *feel*—it all, so differently from you. Excitement, courage, self-forgetfulness showed you but duty in the grand charge you made on that terrible team; but my heart stood still, for I realized the peril to—a friend!"

"The peril was to several friends," he answered gravely. "Surely most to that brave boy, clinging to reins that dragged under the very heels of the brutes; and—to her."

Miss Moore's brown eyes, gazing straight ahead so softly, came quickly to "Left!" and the little hands unclasped and dropped sharply to "Attention!" as the man went on, rather absently:

"I never saw cooler courage anywhere. Lifted bruised and breathless from the wreck, her first gesture was to lift the weight from him, even before she had voice to cry, 'Is he killed?'"

"Of course the romance were unfinished without a heroine." The woman's voice began coldly, quick-warming to tenderness, as it continued: "And I told you a week since, on this very spot, that Dalia was one in soul!"

"You were right in that as in other things you said of her," Latour answered to her words, rather than their meaning. "She is her father's daughter!"

"Do you believe she loves him?"

The question came suddenly; his surprise at it turning the man's face to hers in real amaze.

"Spofford Cushing! No more than I believe—well, that you love Robbie Pluffer," he answered, half at random. "I do not believe that woman in soul, but veriest child in heart, dreams of loving any man but her father. The love she may find some day must be her master, and women like her must recognize mastery through trial—as she could never have done—before they yield to it, unknowing!"

"You judge us keenly," the woman said, raising eyes full to his, but quickly dropping them again. "Oh! how we wrestle with that feeling, only to have it master us at last! But you are right; it was providential." She led him deftly away from the dangerous ground of personality, giving a little shudder. "Think what a parting this night's had been, with *one* of you five in peril killed or mangled!" She turned her face to the moon-brightened East; her voice low and tremulous. "And the parting to most of us is heavy enough. You leave for South America at midnight?"

"How in the deuce did you know that?" his surprise answered inwardly the sudden query; for he had told no one but Dale and his wife. But his lips responded quietly:

"Yes, by way of San Francisco."

"I have often wondered if your ranche interests out there satisfy you as others might, found nearer home. They mean mastership, wild freedom, much to a man like you, I often think; but such a man owes somewhat to country—friends." She spoke slowly, absently, looking far over the water; quickly interrupting herself —"Pardon my forgetting the youth of our renewed acquaintance, General Latour; but this living under tents does bring people closer together! Well"—there was bare suspicion of a sigh in the exclamation—"I trust you will not so nearly have forgotten me, *next* time we meet."

"You are unjust; but I hope the interval will not be so long," the man answered courteously, as he turned, resting on his cane and looking absently over the water, streaked with one clear ripple from the just risen moon.

" I shall not soon forget *that;* nor any of the nights on this rare old shore ! "

" I shall ever keep its memory, as we see it now ; just enough cloud to hint the silver soon to broaden out," the woman said, softly, feelingly. " Thus I shall keep near me the absent—*friends,* who leave us for the North to-night."

A quick flash of the black eyes toward her had shown the dangerous gap in time, and she took it without a break in the pace.

" A courteous reminder," he answered. " My luggage has gone, but there are many last words to be spoken and—hear !—taps."

Walking cottageward, Bella Moore spoke in friendly frankness of her plans; a visit to her cousin, Lady Varicœur, for the London season; then the Scotch lakes and a winter in Italy, for art and music. And now, just within the gate, she paused and spoke more seriously, the moon just reaching them under the giant oaks sentineled there.

" We have become good friends," she said low but distinctly, " and *I* shall recall these days with pleasure. I would have you do the same, but we, of the world, are so subject to misconstruction. I know you never break a promise. Will you make me one ?"

" To wear your colors? Yes ! To ride for you in the lists, against all comers ? I swear it ! " he answered lightly, to hide perplexity.

" Neither, but to do something harder than either." Her voice trembled slightly now. " I rarely ask a grace of man, or woman ; I beg of you a favor—and justice."

" To yourself, even if not to your sex, I could refuse

neither," Latour replied earnestly. "You have my pledge to—"

"To judge me now and always as *you* find—as *you* know me! Here—abroad—I may be misjudged by—" speaking earnestly, rapidly, she hesitated but an instant— "perhaps by some we both love best! You had forgotten the awkward girl you met me first; but, since that day, I have watched your career—respected your fame. I would have you—until *your own* eyes see me otherwise—respect me as more than the mere worldling you hear me called!"

Had Adrien Latour been cradled on Bunker Hill and weaned on the East wind, he had not been proof against that musical voice, pleading for justice to her better self. But his French blood, already warmed by sympathy of taste, moved faster than its wont under spell of Southern night and odor-laden air; so he answered promptly to the tremulous tones:

"You have my pledge!"

"It is a compact; and you "—she held out her hand— " will be loyal to it?"

For the second time that week—the first in many a year, and under wide-variant impulse—the Creole bent and pressed his lips upon a woman's hand. But this time he added the words:

"I will be loyal and true, always!"

The hand, still lightly resting in his own, was hastily withdrawn. Simultaneously, a step crunched on the shells behind him, as Miss Moore exclaimed:

"Naughty boy! You should not monopolize her this last evening!"

Then Latour, resting on his cane, thought Dalia's

voice sounded strangely dry and hard as it came over his shoulder in answer:

"Mr. Pluffer was kind enough, Miss Moore, to help Spofford on his way back to papa's tent. And mamma asked me, should we meet, to remind you that we all rise at dawn."

At the cottage porch, Mrs. Winston added her little lecture to Bennie Everett's, for desertion of the errant pair; reproaches which Bella Moore accepted with downcast eyes and cheeks that had seemed, in stronger light, unduly pale. Latour answered with easy persiflage, but his eyes sought vainly to question Dalia's for some betrayal as to her having seen the little comedy of chivalry enacted at the gate. But the girl was placidly bidding adieu to Robbie Pluffer, who had shaken hands from the elbow with all the party and now, at the step, spoke low and earnest words of farewell to her.

As his dog-cart rattled away into the darkness, Latour asked:

"Will you not sing once more, before we all part?"

"I think I can not sing," she answered with unwonted hesitance. "The night dampness and—but I'll play something, if you wish." And she passed abruptly into the parlor, lit only by dim reflection from the low moon. But the practised fingers needed no sight to aid them and she played brilliant, strong movements with firm touch.

"I believe Dalia plays better to-night than I ever heard her," Miss Moore said, breaking the long and enjoyed silence. "That interpretation is simply perfect."

"Yes; we feel her music more, perhaps, because she

does," Latour answered. "That is my favorite of all ballads she——"

He stopped abruptly; the player doing the same in mid-bar. She had dropped into quieter themes; and last, very softly and dreamily, into the very soul of Goring Thomas' ballad. The low, rich melody was phrased clearly to the final thought—only a moment's break as the piano sang:

> " My heart was weary and oppressed
> With some strange longing, unconfessed—
> Ah! Night of love ——"

Suddenly the keys were silent. Next instant Dalia stood in the shadow of the doorway, saying very quietly:

"I am going up, Miss Moore, if you are ready."

But it was Latour who first moved to her side, as he said:

"I thank you for your music to-night, more than ever. I hate to say good bye, little girl, for who knows how long. But the echo of that song will come to me across the pampas, until—we meet, somewhere."

## CHAPTER XVI.

### FOR THE FUTURE.

The ladies had withdrawn from the porch, the matrons to Mrs. Everett's room, for last additions to trunks already overful; the maidens to Dalia's bower upstairs. There, primly strapped trunks stood ready, and the girl, already in her traveling dress, sat down with a book, while her senior moved to the window and, leaning against the frame, gazed out thought-engrossed into the moonlight. Neither had spoken since the rencontre at the gate, and Miss Moore's tact was all at fault, as to whether Dalia had seen the Creole's action, or overheard his words. But, as she listened in vain for Dalia's hand to turn a leaf of the book, she felt an armed truce to be her best attitude for the time. The hum of voices—now strident, now indistinct—floated up from the wide gallery below and she knew that Latour was saying his last words to his old comrade; that her last to him, for the present, had been spoken.

"And, sorry as I am to part, Dale," Latour was saying, unheard by the woman, "I am rather glad all this thing is over."

"Yet it has done a good work," Everett answered decidedly, "perhaps a great one."

"Well, I confess to shirking duty," was the reply, "but I saw very little instruction——"

"But there was some of the best drilling I ever saw," his friend broke in. "Some that would have shamed the first company at the Point, when you were captain."

"Um—yes; on fine points," Latour rejoined. "But you did not bring a brigade of mustangs a thousand miles, Dale, and pin printed ribbon on them—for points."

"You are right; I did not!" The Federal General rose to his feet and spoke gravely. "I did that, as I would again do it to-morrow, to let these men from far Northwest and far Southwest—the Creoles and the Hoosiers—the Georgians and Minnesotans—learn, of their own experience, the great truth they now know; that truth which none who think with me could have taught them in a cycle, by word of mouth; which no shrieking extremist can lie them out of now!"

"You *are* a grand old fellow, Dale!" Latour rose too, and put both hands on Everett's shoulders. "That great heart of yours is as loyal and big—yes, as young, to-night, as when we were *plebs* at the Point? Old friend and comrade, I believe I am mean enough to—envy you!"

"What keeps me young, dear old boy?" Everett's hands went up, old-day fashion, and clasped the two strong ones on his shoulders. "With such wife and child, with God's blessing on our home—yes, Ad, and with a country!—why should I not feel life worth living?"

"Yes; *you* have everything to live for," Latour said gravely, dropping his hands and turning away.

"And you might have," the Puritan answered. "This country is yours, as well as mine. Its fairest, most heaven-endowed section is yours! What it needs alone is men like you; and yet you leave it, to waste the wealth, the genius God has given you on aimless chimeras! Adrien, what you should have is a home—a wife!"

The Creole turned away abruptly: "I am too old to think of that," he said gloomily.

"You are younger, more vigorous than most men of thirty," Everett rejoined. "A man of forty-six, with no gray in his mustache, who rides through glass sash to rescue maidens, can not plead exemption by age!"

"You speak from the man's standpoint, not the woman's," Latour answered bitterly. "Do not discuss this, Dale. 'Tis utterly useless. I shall die the last of my race! It is written—and I am Turk enough not to rebel."

"Nonsense," retorted the Northerner. "This week proves that my standpoint *is* the woman's. No youth, from either side of the line, has been so sought."

"There was only one major-general, in mufti," the Creole answered gravely. "You know I would want no woman who would marry my shoulder straps, or my money!"

"No *woman* would!" was the prompt retort. "Why that toast of the city and the camp, Bella Moore——"

"This is the last night together, Dale!" Adrien Latour turned suddenly and faced his friend in the moonlight, now sifted through the leaves in shining spangles of silver. "Possibly we may never meet again, and I wish to say something as though we were really parting at the gates of death. I will never marry. This week, perhaps more than all my past, makes me sure of that! I have long intended what I now tell you; before I start

for the pampas this time I shall make my will, naming
Dalia as my heir."

"Adrien! This is—"

"Wait! What else should I do? There is no Latour, no d'Auvigne left. I have one brother—one sis-
ter in all the world. God's law is higher than man's
law, but if they bury me yonder, who will voice the
dead man's wish—that *their* daughter should have what
is his, not for its worth, but for the love that wills it."

"I understand you, Adrien," Dale said, deeply moved,
"but I have plenty for those dear ones. If I be not rich,
yet they will never lack aught."

"You are a public man, Dale, a business man in some
sort. With you Yankees, stocks and bonds and banks
vanish like mist," the other answered, hiding deep feeling beneath a smile. "Wall street and Canada are too
near neighbors to you, Dale; but plantations, levee-
blocks, and ranche-lands can not melt. There are pleasanter things to talk of. My mind is made up, nothing
can change it."

"Nothing, Ad?"

"Nothing—" He paused an instant and his voice
lowered. "Nothing *possible!*"

Then those two, knowing one another so well, talked
far toward midnight; hearing the distant scream of the
southbound locomotive, scurry and roar as the train
rushed through the cut above. That brought Bennie to
the porch and Colonel Winston from the camp.

"Good-bye, Dale! Good-bye, Bennie! God bless
you both!" in the clear voice of the Creole.

"Good bye, dear old fellow!"

"Good bye, Adrien! Write often; you promised!"

9

came in duet from the Everetts; hands were clasped in
loving farewell; and the Creole strode away with
Colonel Winston, through the wood's path to the railroad
crossing.

Under the table lamp, Dalia sat quietly; never raising her eyes from the book, as the voices rose on the
night wind and floated clear through the vine-trellised
window.

But Bella Moore, leaning against the window frame
in trailing cashmere that made the grand curves of her
figure a white statue, save for heavy masses of dark
hair, loosened to the night wind, noted that the leaf
never turned; that the gaze of the steady eyes fell
beyond the page. Yet, as the words of farewell passed
the window, the breeze that bore them to Dalia carried
also a whispered contralto tone — the vocal ghost of a
" Good bye! "

A moment more—as the striding figures, never looking back, were lost in gloom of woods—she caught
a smothered sob; and looking up, saw the white
statue wide-eye, tense—one hand pressed to its heart,
the other extended in almost caressing gesture of farewell! Then, ere she could speak, the older woman
had glided to her side, slid gracefully to the floor and
buried her head in the young girl's lap, as she sat stiffly
still, a cold surprise upon her pale, pained face.

So one minute—two, and still no word was spoken,
when Miss Moore raised her now flushed face to the
white, wondering one of the younger woman. But under the scrutiny of those gray eyes the woman of the
world blushed deeper still, rising and turning her face
aside.

"Forgive me, Dalia, I was weak, childish! I am as ashamed of myself as you must be of me!"

"Why should *I* be ashamed?" Dalia's voice was cold, monotonous, and she stood still, but erect.

"Because—" The brown eyes sought the floor under steady gleam of the gray, felt if not seen. "Because—"

"What? I simply do not understand."

For once Bella Moore lost her self-possession. Whether that she was not understood, or that she did not wish to be, she cried hastily:

"Because you do not wish to! Because you know that he is unworthy that either of us should regret!"

The Puritan girl still gazed quietly and gravely at the hot, downcast face of the brilliant woman before her, but her lips straightened their line and the voice rang hard as clear that answered:

"Pardon my dullness, equally my want of interest. But I do *not* know of whom and what you speak."

"You do not know Adrien Latour's past!" The woman was amazed now; or else her acting was a revelation of art. "*You* ignorant of his life in Paris!—that beautiful artist's model—"

"Pardon me again!" Dalia broke in; not hastily, but with decision that brooked no question. "I only know that General Latour is the oldest and dearest friend my father and mother have; that he is still their guest, under this roof! If I hear anything of him from *any one*, it should be from them!"

The cashmere folds over Miss Moore's bosom rose and fell rapidly; her hands pressed together in quick, sharp clasp, as the hot color fell slowly from her face. But when she spoke — raising gently-pleading eyes to the calm ones, never moved from her face—the old rich voice was there, tremulously sweet:

"Dalia! all of us are weak sometimes, but that is poor excuse. Your loyalty shames me more than words may tell! Dear, *will* you forgive me?"

"*I* have nothing to forgive," Dalia answered with perfect courtesy, that had a savor of Boston fog in it. "But as we all rise at reveillé, I must keep you up no longer. Good night!"

And it may have been the fog that prevented her seeing—as she turned to her own room—the pretty, dimpled hand extended to her.

## CHAPTER XVII.

### THE OLD HOMESTEAD.

Three years have passed since that June night under the magnolias; full, busy years to most of those met there; freighted, for some of them, with trial and disappointment.

Miss Moore had gone to her cousin, Lady Varicœur, and London had promptly accepted the graceful and accomplished woman as the best American type. Rumor had later come that she might have become a princess during a winter at Rome, and more recently newspapers and private letters had noted her renewed triumphs in London, hinting that more than one titled Briton would be left, as was Lord Ullin, on the shore when she should sail for home. And now, it was said, a noble lord—a widower who had long been a recluse from court—would follow her to America and claim her hand. Often, in those years, the belle had written to the Everetts, but Dalia, when at home from her studies, had insisted that Miss Moore was her mother's friend and that matron, Roman only in great matters, had replied for both of them.

But Dalia had not lost her Southern friends, she and Mrs. Winston keeping up a regular correspondence, aided by not infrequent postscripts from the Colonel; and Bessie Brooke sent frequent missives in rigidly square envelopes, addressed in huge, running hand. And no Christmas, Easter or other festal date, in those

three years, had lost Robbie Pluffer opportunity for
boxes of *bons-bons*, books or decorated cards, all acknowledged kindly, in just such notes as made excuse
for no guerrilla correspondence.

Dalia had been much of the time in New York and
Boston, improving her voice and perfecting her playing.
The voice had improved proportionately to the physical
and mental development, showing as she now neared
her twentieth birthday. And it was only development,
not change; all the higher and better traits of the girl
mellowed in the woman; while keenly-marked peculiar-
ities had but rounded their sharp edges, from friction
against cultivated people of the metropolis and "the
Cambridge set." Now the limited circle, male and
female, to which she restricted her intimacies, found
the rich, thoughtful face and splendid physique were
but indices of rarer gifts within. And yet, Bennie
Everett confessed—though only to herself—that Dalia
had changed in some indescribable way. Loving, selfless and devoted to both parents, as when a child, she
still seemed reticent of deeper feelings, at times; and the
watchful mother-eye detected frequent shades of sadness which were hidden wholly from the great love and
clear sight of the father.

That father, too, had tested—in small annoyances and
great troubles—the full strength of his child's devotion;
the full reliance to be placed upon her clear judgment
and brave acceptance of disaster. For when called
suddenly home, cutting short cherished studies at mid-
moment most essential; when—worst of all—compelled
to forego that year in Germany with her mother, which
had been the Mecca of her life-dream, Dalia not only

failed to murmur, but rose above disappointment more cheery and equable than she had been for many a month.

For Dale Everett, through long army and public life, had made many friends and incurred some obligations. Never speculative, his open habit and generous impulses made swift recognition of both claims upon him; and, easily prosperous in his Western home, he answered the call of friends with the same freedom that met the wants, real or imagined, of his little family. Endorsements for large amounts had successively fallen back upon him; had been promptly settled at heavy sacrifice of securities, leaving him greatly cramped for means.

His was not the nature to yield to ill fortune; nor could it brook outlay beyond income, his horror of debt equaling that of dishonor. So, home expenses were curtailed, Dalia recalled from the East and the German tour abandoned, apparently forever. But, gravest disappointment of all, a long cherished scheme to rebuy the old homestead on the Hudson had just become possible to accomplish. The death of Mr. Mason's creditor, who had foreclosed during the war, but refused every overture made later, left his heir willing to sell "for a fancy price." This had not deterred the doting husband, Bennie's heart being set on the old home all their married life. And now, with the prize in easy grasp, fortune dashed it from his hand.

Through all this, no complaint had ever come from the real helpmeet at his side; and the cheery, useful presence of his daughter brightened the reduced home as no wealth could have done.

With Adrien Latour—first in South America; later in England and Italy—the Everetts had kept up correspondence, strangely regular on his part; Dalia only sending or receiving messages, declaring that studies, or employment, prevented writing any one. From Latour, they knew that he had met Bella Moore in London and Rome; though the letters of that wise virgin chanced not to note the fact. And, from Bennie, Latour learned of the long-coveted acquisition of Rose Villa; soon after, hearing from Dale of that bitter disappointment and its cause. His prompt and brotherly offers of assistance had been declined, as unnecessary.

So the united little family, in its Western home, was warmed by love and friendship, as Christmas came; bringing Robbie's unfailing greeting and a box larger than ever. Another box from the South, rough and cumbersome, was glorified by reminiscence; for the Winstons sent red-berried holly, flowering bamboo, mistletoe and the graceful gray moss from their Gulf forests. The season, too, brought frank letters and books of new music from Spofford Cushing; still calmly devoted to the woman, as he had been to the girl, but ever restrained from speaking what he felt most. For Dalia, free, generous and gentle, yet treated "Major Cushing"—the rising young lawyer on the Governor's staff—as she had ever treated "Spofford."

One friend, however, usually most thoughtful and always most valued, sent neither word nor token at Christmas-tide; and—whatever husband or wife might have thought of negligence, more marked in this than in prosperous years—loyalty to friendship, no less than consideration for each other, prevented any reference to the lapse. Only Dalia had remarked, by seeming chance, when her mother bade her:

" Drape Uncle Ad's picture with some of Mrs. Winston's moss and holly, daughter. "

" You have no letter from him, mamma ; have you ? "

" He is such a Bedouin, daughter ; and foreign mails are so irregular. We will hear in a day or two."

And the girl, twining the graceful gray festoons about the speaking likeness of the Creole, had only answered aloud :

"Perhaps. It would please you and papa." But as the clear black eyes gazed from the pictured olive face into her own, a bitter, rebellious defiance rose from her heart to her lips ; crushed back to inward utterance only : " Has he really two lives ? One that he lives in the home of his friends ; one in that of—the model ! "

And, at that quiet, happy Christmas dinner, when other good friends had been remembered, Dale Everett filled full the glasses on his left and right, saying heartily :

" Now, to our best of friends ! "

Dalia raised her glass dutifully, but the one little sip of sherry seemed strong enough to jump deeper color to her cheeks, though she spoke no word.

Then, days gliding swiftly by in that still-contented home, brought Dalia's birthday and the last of the year ; for the girl had been born on the anniversary of that snowy one, when her mother's loyal hand had sought that of her unselfish lover, with the words : " Until death do us part ! "

Dalia was at the piano, deep-absorbed in the weird, boldly-grouped harmonies of Grieg, when her father's call summoned her to his cosy study across the hall. By his chair, with her hand resting on his shoulder and her blue eyes tear-dimmed, Mrs. Everett still showed a not unhappy face. Dale held an open letter, its large envelope, heavy with prim, business-looking documents, lying on the desk.

"Dalia, this letter to me is meant for you," he said earnestly, as the girl ran in, obedient. "It is very brief, but it means—very much!"

Spite of her will, the voice Dalia tried to control would not come. The color, left in her face by sympathy with Grieg's quaint thought, fell from it as she stared at her father without reply. Without one glance at the letter she knew it was from Latour; and what in it could "mean much" for her!

"It is a great surprise to your mother and to me," he went on gravely. "But we both hope from our hearts that you may receive its offer as we do."

Will conquered so far that the girl's pale lips forced out the words:

"Oh! papa—if—"

Then they closed firm and straight; but no will could keep back the surge of crimson that swept cheek, brow and neck, as the firm, white hand closed on the chairback, with a grip almost fierce. And the mother's eyes, seeing through their mist of tears, could not comprehend; and Dale's were on the letter, as he read:

"DEAREST FRIEND: My lacking Christmas greeting to you and yours was, in part, from 'the law's delay;' in part, from preference to ask my first serious favor from Dalia on her birthday. A lucky chance put my lawyer in possession of Rose Villa, where so many happy memories of youth are held for us all.

"The title deeds only reached London this week; but

what could an old Bedouin do with a villa on the Hudson? So it struck me that my English notary, who knows none of you, might still put Dalia Everett, spinster, in possession by full transfer. I know Dalia well enough to hear her exclaim, at this distance: ' I will not!' but I also know your clear, good sense, Dale; and I solemnly remind you of our last talk under the magnolias. So explain the business end in your own way, dear old man; and tell Dalia she is taking a real incubus from my shoulders. God bless you all in the coming year, and in all the years to come. Thine as ever, AD.

" *P. S.* I propose to cross in May; so, if the old place has not tumbled down, and *if* Dalia Everett, spinster, will permit, I may pay it a little visit this summer."

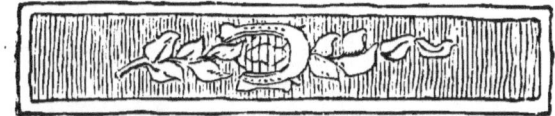

## CHAPTER XVIII.

### INTROSPECTIVE.

Bennie Everett reached over and pressed her lips softly on her husband's forehead, as he drew the formidable-looking papers from their envelope and spread them on the desk before him. But Dalia stood erect and motionless, her hand gripping the chair-back, and all color gone from her face.

"These papers are all in form," Dale said, quietly. "It was very delicate, too, to have the transfer made over there, where he has residence, to save prying eyes here. Wife, your wish is granted; the old homestead can be your home again!"

He turned to Dalia, her mother's eyes also seeking her face for answer.

"Papa! Mamma! I—*can not!*" The girl tore the words from her lips; but, once opened, the feeling that mastered her swept by those portals of speech, low, but vehement: "It would be indelicate—wrong—feeling as I feel, knowing what I know!"

"What you know!" Dale began in wonder; adding, quickly: "But, of course, you can not suspect what he said there, for I never told even your mother."

"I have no idea what he—what *you* were told," the girl answered, slowly and decisively. "But I will not accept this gift!"

"I feel that you could not accept it from any one else," her father returned, calmly, "but it is different, from him."

"I can not accept it—from him! Papa, I know how I wound you both! I feel how much happiness I take from mamma! But I am your daughter and I *must*—refuse!"

"You never act without reason, Dalia," the father argued gently. "Here you can have but one, the value of the gift. To me, *that* counts for no more than Robbie's *bons-bons*, or Spofford's music. The intent alone gives value to any gift; and I would not have Adrien dream that you even hesitated!"

"I do not hesitate," she answered as promptly as coldly. "I have decided!"

"This is impulse; the sudden surprise, Dale," the mother said; coming to the girl and passing a loving arm around her. "Come, daughter; if you have a reason, you can tell it to your mother."

"I have nothing to tell," Dalia answered coldly; not changing her pose. "I may be unreasonable, as you say, papa; but I insist on declining this gift!"

Dale Everett's lips came together in rare compression; but his eyes, while fixed steadily on his child's face, had no unkindness in them. There was regret, but not reproach, in the tone that said:

"You are a woman, daughter; not a child, now. If I could, I would not coerce your judgment; but, in some things, mine may be more reliable. For reasons I can not explain now, there is no shade of indelicacy —not one touch of obligation even—in this proffer. Were there either, you know your father had not let it reach you. On the contrary, Dalia, it is not only right and just that you accept; but refusal would shame your father beyond expression—would mortify his generous friend of a lifetime, even more!"

"Papa!" There was a world of obsecratory pathos in the one word. Then the girl added very calmly: "Mamma was right. This is very sudden! Let me think of it!"

She turned gravely from the room, ascending to her own. Dale quietly folded the papers and locked them in his desk; and his wife, taking the cue of her action from his, as was her wont, went quietly after her wraps for an evening drive. Both had always left Dalia's affairs to her own judgment; and both now felt that she would decide as she deemed to be right, even at risk of direct disobedience.

In her own room, Dalia Everett walked straight to the mirror and looked long and steadily into her own reflected eyes. Over her face, at first deadly pale, changes swept in quick procession; earnest questioning—painful doubt—hot flushes, whether of anger, or shame—again a half smile, showing only in indicated dimples, while the lips were firmly still. Gradually the face softened to its natural grave placidity; the soft flush of healthful body returning with healthful state of mind. But through all that rigid scrutiny of self, the girl looked bravely into her own eyes; never flinching under their accusation or reproof. And at last, that strange, strong character, which sought few friendships and not one confidante, came out in words; epitome of bitter struggle and supreme conquest.

"What am I, to judge!" she said aloud. "Why should I dare to set a life of devotion to those I love—a revelation of manhood and gentleness to myself—aside for strange, half-spoken words of hers! Dalia Everett, I am ashamed of you!"

She turned lowly from the mirror, her face placid but resolved; quietly finished her toilet and went down to the piano. She began to think with her fingers. Dreamy, sad at first, the nocturnes glided into stronger themes; till, letting those firm, absolute hands do their own will, they fell into the Rubenstein *motif* she had first played on the Gulf-side—how many years ago?

Over the clear whiteness of her face gradually spread a soft, rosy glow; the eyes deep-set in dreamy memory; the firm lips softening, now and again, into a smile half-sad, half-happy. But flush and smile both deepened, as the fingers—of their own will seemingly—moved into the well-known song; and the low, rich voice hummed softly :

> "My heart was weary and oppressed
> With some sweet longing ——— "

Hoofs without, upon the snow; an opening door and unwrapping in the hall; then the mother and father entered the parlor. The girl's voice was stilled; but the clear, white fingers touched the keys, very softly, as she spoke, without turning :

"Papa, mamma was right. I should be ungracious—unworthy of your daughter—did I wound him by refusal. Write at once to"—only an instant's hesitation—"Uncle Ad, and thank him for me, in your own good way. And now, papa, kiss your little girl for her birthnight, and what it has brought to her!"

Strong hands, but infinitely tender, were laid upon her shoulders, as the father bent down and kissed the upraised lips. Then, as the mother's gentle arms crept round the girl, and the soft-caressing cheek

pressed the love-mantling one of youth, Dale Everett
said :

"Your decision should have been ours, daughter.
But you have made us very happy that it will delight,
not mortify, the great-hearted gentleman who honors
so few by proffer of his friendship."

The white hands were running over the keys once
more; very softly now and making scarcely audible the
refrain of the song.   Over its low, soft plaint came
the girl's voice, low and soft as well :

"And tell him, papa, that we will force him to
become 'Indian giver' if he fail to come to us in
June !"

## CHAPTER XIX

Time stays his flight for " man, nor woman neither."
Summer had come again, finding the Everetts in pleasant occupancy of Rose Villa, far from injured during
their interval of exile. For the canny holder of the
property had justified his added valuation by constant
repair and beautifying addition.

Dalia occupied the rooms of her mother's girlish days;
opening on her studio, where finished pictures on the
walls, or studies yet upon the easel, showed much
originality and creditable breadth of handling. But
every one of them evinced haste to reach result, rather
than that finesse which alone makes finished work.
So the studio stood rather as memoranda of bold talent
than of the close and patient labor, without which even
genius may soar far and yet accomplish nothing. And
while her painting showed the only want of thorough-
ness in any of Dalia's attempts, she frankly confessed it;
declaring to her father that she thought too fast for hand
to follow.

" It is so different with music," she would deprecate,
though more in defiance than regret. "Fingers may fly
along the keys in perfect sympathy with thoughts, rush
upon us as they may! There, reward of perfected expression keeps pace with the idea, placid, weird, bizarre,
tender as it may be. If a tone seems false to thought,
that corrects itself in consonance. But with the brush,

10

one false tone applied in haste kills all value of inexorable idea, until it is wiped out, the just one applied and—
inspiration gone! Without that, drudgery begins and
good work is impossible. I know it is different, papa,
where eye and hand move in twinned perfection toward
accomplishment; but that is genius, and I know I am
only a—dauber! I never, never will accomplish one
tithe in color that I may in sound!"

Still, the wish of fond parents being her only law of
life, Dalia painted on, and honestly as she might; yet
finding time, on certain days of the week, to drill a large
class of younger neighbors in her improvised but well-
equipped gymnasium.

And with all that, she made time for one pet pupil in
music, whom she volunteered to teach; a tall, swarthy girl
whose natural gift and hard labor had made her a fair
pianist, with indurated faults that would rise defiant over
good taste and earnest effort.

"I do not mean to give Dolly up, mamma," Dalia had
declared. "She has character, mind and ambition that
spurs her to work, which would make a richer girl great.
I should be what Cedric, the Saxon, called *nidering*, not
to give the little time and care sure to correct her faults.
Dolly has good piano hands; better, the true musical
soul; and the few hours a week I spare to help her out
may fit her to help herself some day."

So, those quiet days of earlier summer had been busy
ones for Dalia; happy ones, too, in that content which
comes to selfless natures from their work for others.
Nor were self-imposed duties neglected, as busier days
came with approaching midsummer; and vicinage to
West Point, and its magnet of "encampment," brought

visitors as in decades gone, when the gentle nature of Bennie Standish had foiled the brilliance of Edith Van der Huysen.

And now the walls of Dalia's studio showed better pictures than before; figures of strength and type, yet unconventional, and all finished with best methods of the life-school. For, early one June morning Bella Moore sat before her easel in rapt mood, and most tasteful gown, protected by jaunty student's apron. And Dalia sat near by, diligent and careful awhile; then resting brush and leaning back to gaze long and earnestly upon that wonderful face on the other's canvas.

Wholly unchanged, yet mellowed in some indefinable way, the firmly soft oval of the older woman's face retained its strange charm of youthfulness. Three years of wearying belleship abroad had left no one line upon the smooth skin; the brown masses of hair rebelled in the same sheen; while the superb figure, if a shade more full, was lithe and graceful as before.

A careless glance had counted the fair girl, plying brush with steady hand, but compressed lip and slightly clouded brow, as elder of the pair; for Bella Moore had somehow found that fabled spring, elusive to search of Ponce de Leon. Her smile was quite as ready, her brown eyes as luminous and speaking, as when she used their masked batteries so successfully at the Gulf side, three Junes gone. But the mobile lips were touched with some tenderness, the eyes reflected some great, inner depth, those other days had never known.

"You are right, Bella, she had a marvelous beauty!" Dalia exclaimed suddenly, gazing intently at the canvas. "And you are doing wonderful work in bring-

ing back the youth and soul-freshness to the face. If
you keep the likeness, that expression will be a triumph."

"It shall be, dear," the other answered softly, never
raising her eyes. "All other portraits were in the pride
of womanhood. This of the girl, untouched by worldliness, must be my best work. Dalia, I am painting it
to surprise—*him*."

Miss Moore had crossed from England the preceding
week, followed by incorporate whispers of conquest
everywhere; and the last "Paul Pry"—a journal with
as many eyes as Argus and many a tongue more than
ancient Rumor—spoke of a solid and embodied nobility
that would soon follow and claim her for himself. Mrs.
Everett—loyal ever to her likings—had promptly sent
mandate for "a good, long visit," ignoring—if indeed
she had noted—Dalia's absolute silence as to the suggestion. And, when Miss Moore arrived at Rose Villa,
the meeting of the two had been easy and unrestrained,
if not affectionate; a want made up by Bennie's real delight and Dale's warm greeting to the woman both ad-
mired and one truly loved.

Dalia had inwardly blessed that somewhat gushing
welcome, punctuated by frequent query; for behind it
she could mass all her forces of self-control. So, inborn
courtesy, aided by hospitable habit, met the graceful
tact and society calm of the guest in a manner quite as
perfect as her own. But the afternoon, full of social
duty, left no chance for *tete-a-tete* between the pair.

Colonel Winston, just relieved from a tour on the
Board of Visitors, brought his wife for their long promised visit to the friends so congenial and so staunch in
the flying years since first met at Mobile.

"I should never have forgiven you, Colonel—never!" Mrs. Everett cried, with extended hand, as the two matrons uncoiled from the inevitable embrace, "had you not brought Sally this time!"

"I am too good a soldier, I hope, ever to desert," the Southerner answered in his suave way, releasing his hand from the husband's cordial grasp to take that of the wife. "But sometimes I surrender, gladly. When inclination spurs, General, no gap is too wide to cover. Ah! Miss Dalia, you could not claim the 'little girl' now, that saved so much boredom in Dixie. But you are not one bit changed; only the perfected promise! And Miss Bella, too! returned the *Venus Victrix!* My dear Mrs. Everett, with these lovely gardens and this vine-clad portico, we need but one face to carry us back to the Gulf shore; that of your 'courier' and Miss Dalia's riding-master!"

The quick flash of Miss Moore's eyes to the girl's face found it quiet and unchanged, only the flush of cordial welcome on it, as she answered quietly:

"An omission to be filled very soon, Colonel, for General Latour will join us next week."

It was Bella Moore's well-trained face that now flushed deeply, but Dalia, catching the unusual glow, covered it quickly from the rest by adding:

"But, Mrs. Winston, your husband makes one serious omission, that genial Mr. Pluffer."

"Not one bit changed, the same old Robbie," Winston laughed back. "He is still as broad as the views of a philanthropist, while deeper than their performance."

"Then you have not heard?" Mrs. Winston quickly offered her budget. "Why, Robbie is engaged. Early in the fall he will be married to pretty Bessie Brooke. The last girl he tried to rush—a stranger from Chicago —proved too strong for Robbie. The poor boy really seemed in earnest, for once; but dear little Bess caught his heart in the rebound and now they are the happiest pair on earth."

"I am so glad," Bennie Everett said earnestly; and Miss Moore—all aplomb once more—thought she caught a strange wistfulness in the mother's eyes as they rested an instant on her daughter's face.

Then baggage came, including Miss Moore's compact painting case; toilets had to be made; and dinner was over before the two younger women—the matrons naturally pairing together, and the gentlemen over their cigars and reminiscence — found themselves alone. They moved slowly down the broad garden walk, as the moon rose above the Hudson, sending silver ripples to the sea; but neither spoke for awhile.

Suddenly Bella Moore broke the silence, quite in her old way of seeming to finish an interrupted sentence; but with something in her rich voice, as new as it was startling to her listener:

"Dalia dear," she said earnestly, but low, "the last time we talked together—that midnight at Mobile—I asked you to forgive me. No; do not speak. You did not dream then—I never dreamed until much later— what real cause I had to ask. I was older than you in actual years; a century your senior in worldliness! I am a proud woman, too, Dalia; but before you to-night —before myself for weeks!—my soul comes to its knees; and I *must* tell the truth before I sleep!"

She caught the deprecating gesture of the other; answering it earnestly:

"No; I did not lie knowingly, perhaps; but my false ideas grew to realities in—in my scheming worldliness. No; let me finish before you speak. Simple girl that you were then—pure woman that you are now! I will risk even your contempt to undo the wrong I then did, unknowing. In my folly, my selfishness, I imagined things that I now know could never have been! I encouraged—half-believed, feelings in my own heart that never did exist! Born in the world; a thorough woman of the world while yet a child—I still had never loved"—her voice grew soft and tender—"*then!* I looked upon a woman's heart, if she had one, as I did upon her face, her fascination, as—a bait! I thought a woman's highest crown"—infinity of scorn crept through the tone—"a brilliant match! It may be reason—it can not be excuse—that I never knew a mother's care, a mother's love!"

And Dalïa, from her heart, answered low:

"It is excuse! I know how great—how real!"

But the other, with only imperious gesture of dissent, went on, evenly but bitterly:

"A chance rencontre, years before; my own false lights then; a chance reply when we first met again gave me wrong suspicions of General Latour—worse thoughts about myself!"

"Stop; you must not speak so!" Dalia broke in; adding gently, "I have forgotten all that—now!"

"I could not forget," Bella Moore went on. "The lie I told you then, unwitting perhaps, surely ignorant, how shameful it was, has upbraided my conscience all these years. It has shamed my womanhood, in all its new-found depths, these past few weeks. Dalia, there

was never a scandal; there was no model! Adrien
Latour was never less than the grand gentleman I could
not understand."

"I know that," Dalia answered gently; but the cer-
tainty in her tone had the solemnity of an oath.

"Let me finish," the older woman said, softly, checking the hand half stretched to touch the girl's arm,
"and then we *may* be friends. Last winter, at Rome, I
met an Englishman—not a society man but a widower
—who cared nothing for women. His heart, they said,
was in the grave of the beautiful, cold, brilliant wife,
lost years before. Chance meeting attracted him to me:
in a week we were friends. Something in my voice
first recalled the wife; traits in me he could not explain,
sympathies none of us comprehend, held him by me.
He was brave, generous, frank; his heart open as the
day. I knew I had waked it from the sleep of memory.
We walked and rode together. One day he told me
what I knew so well, that he loved me!" The woman's
face grew rosy, radiant in the moonlight. "And, Dalia,
for the first time in all my thirty years, I found I *had* a
heart! I loved him then; I am another woman now."

"I am so glad," Dalia's murmur was low, but heart-
born, "that I forgave you last New Year! *So* glad
that you now prove that I was right!" She stood still
and held out her hand.

"Wait! let me finish," the other answered. "Then,
give me your hand, if you can! Later, in London, he
urged me to marry him; showed me the portrait of his
wife. She was, he said, the early friend of your
mother, your father, of General Latour. Dalia, she
was—the model!"

The dead silence was broken only by the tap of little feet upon the gravel. Thought was very busy in both brains. Not unpleasant thought, seemingly, as the faces again came into the moonlight. Then Bella Moore halted, facing the other woman.

"That night, out of hollow, mocking spirit, I asked you to forgive me! Now, out of my full-shamed contrition, I beg it once again!"

Her voice trembled; she raised her great brown eyes full to the girl's gray ones. They filled with rarely-known tears, as Dalia held out both hands.

"Had you sinned," she said gently, "contrition would demand forgiveness. You only erred; so I repeat, I have nothing to forgive!"

Then the lithe, white arms gleamed in the moonlight, as they crept gently about the other's neck!

## CHAPTER XX.

### THE WORLD AND THE FLESH.

So, two women sat in the studio that bland June morning; last touches from the hand of one bringing to the wonderful face of Edith Van der Huysen, that youthful glamour which had swayed men, in many lands.

A week had passed. Latour's advent had produced neither jar nor change in the pleasant party at Rose Villa; for he had dropped naturally into its ways and showed those lazy old ones of his own, quite unchanged. Dalia had received him with a slight reserve, born perhaps from pricking conscience at doubt of his truth, so long uncondoned by herself. And Miss Moore's manner had been frankly cordial, while more quiet than he remembered it before. Host and hostess were equally rejoiced at return of their truant friend; and the Winstons showed that they liked the man and were proud of the representative Confederate.

"I can paint no more, Bella," cried Dalia, tossing down her brush, as she rose and stood behind the other. "It will not come! Your portrait is done; and he must be pleased with it. Even I, who never saw her, feel the power of that face; the magic of those wonderful eyes! I have kept your secret loyally; but you will show it to mamma to-day?"

"I would like her opinion of it; and your father's," was the reply. The artist stepped back; keenly criticising her own work, through half-closed lids. "But

let us take a turn in the garden and get the cobwebs out
of our brains, before lunch."

On a bench, cool-nooked under trees and overlook-
ing the river, the two new friends sat for long and
earnest talk. Bella Moore's nature, once unlocked to it,
seemed to yearn for the sympathy of the strong, fresh
nature of the younger woman. She spoke freely of her
plans and hopes; of her fears that Lord Martindale
might find her less worthy than he deemed of that great
new love she had awakened; but avowed her full intent
that a life of truest wifehood should reward him and
condone, as far as might be, her wasted past. So, selfish
as young love ever is, she had talked on; and Dalia had
listened quietly, but with deep interest. Once and again
the gray eyes wandered from her friend's face, gazing
dreamily, wistfully over the water. But, if she built any
castles in Spain, they were of card-house design, for her
strong common sense toppled them with lightest touch
and she came back to vicarious reality, sometimes with
almost a start; once, or twice, with something near a
sigh.

Meantime, the three old friends, left to themselves by
the Winstons' drive over to a neighbor's, talked earnestly
in the well-remembered old library.

"Yes, I can frankly say I have never seen any girl
improve so, and yet, I could not analyze the change,"
Latour was saying. "I left her a child, Dale; a bright,
strong-natured one, I grant you, but a child still. I
find her now a stately, grand woman, who would grace
any society I know, and yet with no loss of that child's
simplicity."

"And with her child's heart unchanged, too," his friend

assented.  "Change and trouble, work and disappointment, touch without hardening her."

"'My strength is as the strength of ten,
    Because my heart is pure.'"

quoted the Creole half-absently.  "By the way, Dale,
you can not tell how your letter re-assured me.  Do you
know I half-dreaded that she might think my proffer of
the old place a trifle intrusive.  Of course, she could
not know that it would be hers some day anyway."

Husband and wife exchanged quick glances, but the
latter came to the rescue with her feminine tact:

"Our daughter could never feel a kindness from you,
Adrien, more an obligation than one from ourselves.
But even I was astonished when Dale explained—for the
first time then, only—what boundless love for us you
had shown by making Dalia your heir."

"But she doesn't suspect—" Latour began quickly,
but finished with a laugh, "but, of course, she can not.
That wonderful fellow, who can keep a friend's secret
even from his wife, would never let it go further.  But
another thing has been troubling me greatly, which *I*
can not arrange."  He was serious now and his brows
came together.  "You must both help me out, for I
know Dalia would never consent, did she dream that I
suggested it."

"Another gift from the fairy godfather?"  Mrs.
Everett's lips smiled; but her eyes held serious query in
them, which he feared boded opposition.

"A very simple matter," he answered.  "I appreciate
the grave disappointment to Dalia—the really serious
loss, at a time of her life, which can never be recalled—

by losing that year in Germany to perfect her music. As all I have is to be hers, why should she not enjoy a fraction of it to present advantage?"

"Why, my dear old fellow, do you not see—" Everett began. But the other broke in with his impulsive way:

"I see now, what I have always said in the South, that letting a man starve while he lives, only to build him a monument after he dies, is arrant folly. We are both pretty tough, Dale. I may live until Dalia is an old maid, or——marries——"

"Dalia will not marry," her mother put in placidly. "She is too wedded to her art and her duties to divorce from them. She cares nothing for the things most attractive to other girls; least of all for men."

Adrien Latour's black eyes shot one keen, penetrating glance at Bennie Everett's open, honest face; but his sole reply was a very French shrug, as he went on, without other note of her interruption:

"What practical common sense tells us she should do, is to use a trifle of what will be hers—when perhaps too late—and go to Germany now. Dale can spare you a few months, in view of what great results the absence would achieve. I tell you, dear old friends, that I have heard pianists of note—professionals of great fame—in many countries, since we parted; and few of them are what your little girl could be. She is a born artist; but America has done all it can for her. A year of great example, high instruction and musical atmosphere in Germany would make her the peer of the best of them!"

"It would be impossible," Dale answered decisively. "She would never consent!'

"She need never suspect!" the other retorted eagerly.

"Knowing what you two know, you must feel that she would merely be using her own. Knowing her, as I think I know her—she would never inquire the details, if you assured her tha     had arranged to have her go, without inconvenic .ce."

"But could we deceive her, Dale?" the mother deprecated. "Never, since she could understand, have we done that; and now—"

"Now, you need not do it!" Latour broke in. "There is one piece of Levee property in New Orleans, for which I am offered to-day thrice its value, for any purpose to which I could put it. It is hers, not mine; and, though idle, I would not sell it, without Dale's advice and consent. One-fourth of its price— the residue invested to better advantage than now— would give this year in Germany, so longed for and so much needed!"

"I know nothing of business, Adrien," Mrs. Everett answered quietly, "but my feelings tell me that we should not do this. You have already heaped obliga- tions——"

"Stop, Bennie!" Adrien Latour was on his feet, erect and grave. "The obligation is all on my side. My brother's child—yours—has given opportunity to do what leaves me more content, more real happiness, than all else in my life beside. Doing that for me, I ask the further favor, that she may be allowed to use a little of her own for what will give her equal happiness; more than that, will give—what my simple act has not done —results and a future." Both his hands were on Dale's shoulders, and his grave eyes, softened and tender, were full on the st     y ones as he added: "Help me to do this, dear old friends, ... count me your debtor beyond words. I am a bad ...ngler, who can not express what he means the most. 1 ...u, Dale, can explain it to Bennie, and arrange this ... ...ur surprise for your patient, unselfish little girl."

He turned abruptly away, lighting a cigar as he crossed the broad porch, and stepped to the gravelled path.

Nearly three decades had slipped past since Lieutenant Latour had lighted his cigar, had crossed that porch, had strolled down that same garden, on just such a summer day. And then, he had walked on with blind eyes to meet his Destiny!

And now, his eyes took in the broad rolling Hudson, hurrying to the sea; the distant haze of foothills, creeping into mountain distance; the scents of flowers and the pipe of birds, no more than they had, in that day long ago. But all the rage of storm that had swept his young face then was absent now from its bronzed manhood—glorified by thought of good deed done already; expectancy for newer happiness in store for the child of her of yesterday.

Just at the turn of the wide walk—the very spot where, that day, he had met the girl who fixed his destiny; whence she had lightly left him, with mocking jest of Merlin and the god-like king!—Latour came suddenly upon the two young women, flushed by sun and earnestness of talk.

Then, in sudden rush of memory, the whole scene of yore rose before his eyes; and with it came the long-forgotten sequence of that meeting—its shock of loss and rage, resentment and remorse: all conjured up by the rich, low tones of Miss Moore's ... ...—the very eyes that smiled beneath her great Gainsborough hat, as she extended her hand and spoke gaily.   For there, in the garish sunlight the woman of his dead past stood before him in the flesh !   The nameless of the Gulf coast was embodied then ; for the eyes, the voice were Edith Van der Huysen's ;  the very words were those she had spoken :

" Welcome, Sir Laggard ! "

With no taint of superstition in him ; with experience of a world's travel and of women in it everywhere, a chilly thrill tingled about the man's heart, before the woman added pleasantly :

" You were late at breakfast ; but we forgive you, do we not, Dalia ? "

Then the pure, placid face beside the brilliant one banished memory's mirage ; he was all the society man once more ; and, without apparent pause, had taken the taper hand extended and was saying :

"Better a laggard at breakfast, Miss Moore, than in love, or at—lunch !   I come to summon you both for that function. "

But, as he spoke, his eyes were on Dalia's face, turned toward the shadow of a slim cedar on the white path before them.

" My sun-dial tells me that your watch is no laggard, " she said pleasantly.   " It is a full half hour before luncheon.   Have the Winstons returned ? "

" *Peccavi !* I confess error ! "   He laughed easily, as he turned back with them.   " They have not ; so I will do penance for my appetite's anticipation in the studio. May I come and criticise your study of 'Remembrance ? ' "

Only at the studio door, Bella Moore suddenly flushed crimson; though Latour and Dalia, deep in discussion of the study, did not note it; nor her quick parting of the portiere aйd passing in before them. But when they entered, one easel was empty and Miss Moore's canvas faced the wall.

There was interesting talk on art; for Latour knew many famous galleries, where he had done more than merely look at pictures. Besides, he had lounged in many Paris studios whose owners had names world-known. Frankly and warmly he praised Miss Moore's painting; making, here and there, keen comment and good suggestion. Of Dalia's he spoke kindly, but even more frankly.

"Your great fault," he said at last, "the one which shows in all you do, is want of patience. Frequently your thoughts are great ones; sometimes their expression begins to approach greatness; then your brush grows restive, wearied seemingly, and you grow crude. Dalia, you have talent certainly; but you paint more with your brain than with your hand."

"The very thing I always tell papa," she replied. frankly. "You understand me better than they do. I never will do a great thing; but I have done one good one—a patient, loving, honest work; a picture of mamma. Wait!"

She ran into her own room, and Latour, scanning the studies on the wall, caught the turned canvas. Without thought, and before his companion could speak, he raised it, placed it on the easel—stood transfixed before it!

For a moment he looked upon the picture with a life-

11

time in his eyes. The bronzed cheeks grew darker; the long mustache drooped from straight-set lips; the brows contracted, beneath which the eyes looked stern and questioning into those of Edith Van der Huysen, as he had seen her first under that very roof. Then the eyes, cold and stern, but piercing still, sought the face of the living woman by him, now crimsoned and downcast, and there was bitter irony in the low voice that carried the words:

"This is another piece of your work?"

The woman's face, quiet but still flushed, was raised full to his, and her eyes, not defiant but fearless, met his without flinching, as she answered low:

"Yes, it is my work, but not in the sense you mean."

"And this is the 'surprise' you hinted to me three years ago?" His voice was cold, with a hard ring in it. "This work of yours does not surprise me, and it also shows as much of 'art' as it does of 'memory,' does it not?"

"Stop and hear me! You shall not misjudge me, as you did then!" Bella Moore cried, almost piteously. "This was not meant for you to see; though I, too, remember my silly—wicked words! None of them here have seen this face painted, Oh! so differently from what I meant then! None of them but Dalia!"

"She has seen it?" His words came quickly; anxious query dominating the scorn in them.

"Yes; she knows all!" Her face was crimson once more; the eyes downcast.

"And you have told her? You know—"

"Only that this woman was once her father's—her mother's friend; was yours!"

" Are you sure that you told her nothing else? Sure that your half-understood insinuations then—"

" Stop, General Latour!" Again the woman faced him bravely; her slender figure drawn to its full height; the color standing in her cheeks, but her eyes meeting his unflinchingly. " I hold your solemn promise; and, spite of yourself, you shall be 'loyal and true' to it! You *shall* know me as I am, not as the world—not as your own suspicion pictures me. Then, you may 'loyal and true' to yourself as well. All I know of that woman, I have told Dalia. All of it I have told you, too"—the color in her cheeks grew deeper, but neither eye nor voice faltered—"except that I know she was once the wife of the true gentleman, in whose great heart I shall strive, all my life, to—replace her!"

Both stood silent an instant; the portiere parted and Dalia gazed from one to the other with wondering eyes. Then Latour spoke, quietly and slow:

" Let me see your portrait, Dalia. Even with a sterner critic, this one of Miss Moore's had done her— full justice."

## CHAPTER XXI.

### TO GERMANY OR ——?

"I believe I am a pretty fair judge of a pretty woman, Sally "—Colonel Winston spoke with the simple serenity of a connoisseur, as he drew off one boot and reached for his slipper—" but, hang me, if Dalia Everett was not a prettier woman at dinner to-night than Bella Moore."

"Men are such geese!" Mrs. Winston's dangerous remark was the more hazardous, from the medium of pins in her lips through which it filtered.

"In the abstract, granted," her spouse replied placidly. "But what suggests particular allusion to the Rome-saving bird?"

"Germany—" More pins prevented more words.

"Now, Sally, if you explain your natural history by geography, I shall never understand."

"The child is just brimming over with content." The force of information promptly ejected the pins. "Bennie told me after dinner that they are going to send her to Germany to finish her."

"Horrible! What unnatural parents!"

"In music, you great goose! General Everett has made a turn, or a coup, or something you men make; and she only told Dalia, as she was putting on that new dress for dinner. Wasn't it lovely?"

"Yes; wholly so," he answered enthusiastically, "though not quite so much of a V as Miss Bella's."

"Prince Winston! If your soldiers could hear you talk such nonsense as you do to me, they would never win prizes any more! You *know* I meant the news!"

"Seriously, Sally, it is 'lovely' and I am delighted," he answered cheerily. "Dalia deserves her good luck. She is a grand girl anywhere; but a queen at the piano!"

"Prince!"—this suddenly after a pause—"Do you think Latour cares for anybody?"

"For Bella Moore? Nonsense, Sally!"

"No; for Dalia. We women see things you men never dream."

Colonel Winston whistled "Captains, take charge of your Companies;" two bars, softly. Then he said:

"Sally Winston, I am glad your daughter still wears cropped hair. Ten years must elapse before you can test your match-making abilities upon her!"

"Very well, sir! I may be wrong, but he certainly does think a great deal of Dalia!"

"So do I, and much in the same way. Why, Sally, Latour himself told me that he had held her on his knee and fed her pap with a spoon!"

"Stranger things have happened," she persisted. "In many things the General is younger to-day than Robbie Pluffer."

"And, in others, Dalia is older than Bessie Brooke? Granted, Sally; but I am sure he will never marry. There were rumors of an early *affaire;* a duel—her death—a sort of 'dead-heart' romance. But, whatever the cause, my knowledge of the man convinces me that he is the most ingrained, indurated bachelor I ever knew!"

" Well, I am rarely mistaken when it comes to—"

" Taps!" promptly cut in the Colonel, and he turned off the gas.

Meanwhile, the pair discussed occupied the parlor below; Dalia at the piano and Latour lounging lazily in a great cane chair. The grand harmonies of the German wizard floated through the wide windows to Dale Everett and his wife, sitting outside in earnest discussion of the happy effect of the good news upon their darling.

An hour before, Bella Moore had slipped away to her own room, carrying a bulky letter, full of foreign stamps and ornamented with a crest, which had arrived in the evening's mail but was left unopened.

" I really believe, Dale," Mrs. Everett said, presently —" that Adrien understands her as well as we do; for, when I told her you had arranged for the trip, she only threw her arms around my neck and cried : ' Dear, good old papa! How he spoils his little girl!'"

"And she asked me but one question : ' Are you absolutely sure, papa, that it is perfectly convenient?' And when I said yes, there was something in her kiss that made me certain I would never have to tell another white lie about the matter."

" What a friend he is! So loyal, so unselfish." Mrs. Everett's voice was tremulous. " Dale, if anything should happen to us, what a guardian he would make for Dalia."

"My dear girl," the General answered lightly; but his hand rested tenderly upon hers—" I have no intention of making you a widow soon; and you are a pretty healthy woman, thank God! But listen! He was right. Few hands can render Wagner like that."

Dalia was playing "Lohengrin." The grand chords of the "March to the Minister" moved from the strong, precise touch in orchestral masses; soon changing to the "Swan Song," purely interpreted and clearly phrased— each note a rounded tone-pearl.

"I am all German to-night!" The girl's white hands rested on the keys; her clear skin aglow, her gray eyes bright with music-warmth.

"It is the king-land of music," Latour answered. "Go on; I never heard you play so well; never felt Wagner so perfectly before!"

"Yet you have been at Beireuth! O! when I hear 'Parsifal' there! I can scarcely wait. I know by heart every one of those photographs you sent mamma!"

"Did I send them to— her?"

"Yes; had you forgotten? As I study those scenes, I can hear those grand voices—the wonderful chorus— You remember this?"

The clean fingers drew the "Chorus of Flower Maidens" from the keys, with power and precision that vocalized it and brought Latour to his feet.

"He is the great Master of his school," he said, standing by the piano.

"Rather say he is the school!" Dalia answered. "As he made it, so none other will illustrate it again!"

"Yes; and none but a German could have done that work," the man said, looking earnestly at the glowing face below him. "While I hold that Italian is the language of opera, I confess Germany holds the soul of harmony."

"And not of melody?" She answered her own query with that intricate theme-song of "The Meister-singer,"

dwelling lovingly on its delicacies, mastering every diffi
culty with ease that seemed nature. Then, unasked,
her hands strayed into the prelude of Schumann's great
sonata. The cunning rendering, with most delicate
shading rising to richest warmth of color; interpretation under the master-touch now thundering in massive-
grouped harmonies, wailing into plaint half-painful with
its freight of meaning, quick rippling back into purest
theme-melody.

It was Latour's best-loved composition of them all.
He had often told her that it moved him as no other
music did; and now his face softened and flushed, but
his eyes moved from the quick-flying hands back to the
meaning face, beautiful now in the reflected glow of
impassioned soul.

"It is perfect!" he exclaimed, with rare enthusiasm,
as the hands stopped still with the last note. "Dalia,
you play better than even I dreamed! What will a
year in Germany not do for you?"

She made no answer, sitting with hands quiet on the
keys, eyes looking far beyond the music-page before
her into the land of revery. Nor was it peopled, seemingly, with what wholly pleased her, for the color slowly
died out of her cheeks, and their dimples smoothed to
gravity. Then, still gazing into space, half-involunta-
rily it seemed, she asked suddenly:

"You quarreled this morning with—Bella?"

"No," he answered frankly, but surprised by abrupt-
ness of the question. "We were never near enough together to get that far apart."

"But once you fancied you might be," she said, as
if continuing thought. Her eyes came back from space,

fixing mechanically on the music. " You thought you
—liked her."

" Miss Moore!" Only the two words, but the refuta-
tion in their tone might have convinced even a jury of
twelve honest men. Still she persisted quietly :

" You were so much with her—there."

" Was I? On my word I have forgotten." There
was no mockery in the words, only deep sincerity ; but
his eyes questioned earnestly the face not turned to him,
but gradually dyeing deep red, from recollection.

" And that last night you—" she bravely fought her
hesitation—" you swore you would be ' loyal and true,
always.' "

Like a lightning flash the forgotten details of that
parting stood before him, and with them bitter words,
scarce to be restrained, rushed to his lips. Had this
woman, thinking only of self, played upon him—worse,
upon this pure, unworldly child? Then, as suddenly
her words of that morning came back, sweeping suspicion before them, and he answered gently :

" I did promise to be loyal and true to a pledge, made
then ; which I had since kept; which I proved only this
day !—a pledge to judge Bella Moore, not as the world
saw her, but as she showed herself to me ! "

" That was like you ! " She turned her face to him,
with the simple words ; but the voice had changed—was
her own again. Then quickly she turned away her face,
flooded with color once more, as she said:

" But you—— I saw you kiss her hand ! "

" Hers was not the only hand I kissed," he said gently ;
a smile playing about his lips, that faded as he added
very low, with half tremor in the tone :

" When I raised the other hand to my lips, they had no words—there was need of none! "

There was silence a moment; Dalia sitting with face downcast and hands listless in her lap; the man looking down upon her with face swept by doubt—perplexity—pain! Then, with a deep breath, he said rapidly:

" Yes; I have faith that the German year, with its opportunities, its models, its atmosphere, will bring you to the side of the great ones, who interpret the Masters for us."

" Perhaps. " The one softly-spoken word was freighted with more of sadness than of doubt; and again her eyes lifted to look out upon the pictures in space.

Presently he said abruptly:

" You will write me of yourself—of your feelings in your new world of music?"

" Papa will tell you "—She came back with a start— " You will come to him often, will you not? "

" I shall be far from here," he answered slowly. " I am going to Africa."

"Africa!" She looked up pale and wondering.

He strode to the window, gazed into the moonlight a moment; then moved back to the piano.

" Why do you go? " The question was low, but earnest.

" God knows! " He answered rapidly, as though the words came of themselves. " To follow Stanley's trail, or find a new one. Perhaps to get rid of this mockery they call civilization—of this greater mockery—myself! "

" But you will come back? " Again the question was very low, very gentle.

"Who knows? It is a long journey; I may never come back!"

"Never come back!" She echoed his words mechanically. "Papa—mamma—know this?"

"No, I scarcely knew it myself, surely, until just now. I wished to see you all before I decided." He drew a deep breath; then asked quietly: "When will you be ready to sail?"

She sat in the same pose; her face downcast, her hands listless on her lap. The voice was scarce audible, but he heard the words:

"I shall not go."

"Not go? Dalia! Think of what you lose!"

"I have thought what I lose—all of it!" Again the voice was low, tremulous; the words seeming to come against her will.

"Dalia," he asked pleadingly, "tell me why you will not go?"

She only shook her head sadly; the face still downcast. But his quick eye saw a tear fall on the listless hand in her lap. His nervous brown hand, so firm about the sabre's hilt, went softly out; but it shook now, as it rested on the little white one.

"Dália! *Will* you not tell me?"

"Why do you go?" Her question was but a whisper, though the hand beneath his did not tremble.

Adrien Latour bent down toward the drooping girl. Twice his lips moved, and twice his voice refused to do the bidding of that firmest will; at last only the whisper:

"Do you not know why?"

Slowly, gently the Puritan's daughter raised to his a

face pale and grave, the eyes brimming with unused tears. But they looked into his own with all the brave sincerity of her race, and no quiver moved the lips that said:

"I am not sure—, I—"

Suddenly she broke down; a crimson flood swept brow and cheek, as she turned away her face and buried it in her hands.

Next instant his strong arm was about her; his dark, earnest face, glorified by new-born feeling, bent close above her fair hair; the crimsoned cheek now resting on his breast.

Presently, the voice that had never failed in the charge trembling now, he spoke:

"Dalia! Can you really ——. Do you ——?"

The pure face—no longer flushed; no longer tearful now—was slowly raised to his; a great rest in it, as she almost whispered:

"You know I do!"

"And you knew it?"

"Ever since our last ride; since first I knew my will had a master!"

"Only your will, Dalia?" His voice was very low.

"Only my will—then!"

The fair head bowed over the keys; the white hands moved over them with low touch, infinitely tender, and they whispered back:

"Hast thou forgotten, love—so soon?"

Steps echoed on the porch. She rose, standing quietly by his side as Dale and Bennie came to the window.

Then, Adrien Latour took her hand in his, and only said :

" Dalia has promised to go to Germany — with me ! "

FINIS.

# CROSS PURPOSES,

## AN EXPERIENCE IN SEVEN STAGES.

### By T. C. De LEON,

*Author of "Four Years in Rebel Capitals," "Creole and Puritan," "Juny," "The Rock or the Rye," etc.*

**Red Line Edition.**  **120 Pages.** **Lithograph Cover.**

### SIX FULL-PAGE ILLUSTRATIONS.

A very good story, well told.—*Savannah News.*
It is illustrated and is very readable.—*Columbus Despatch.*
Healthy reading that we commend to all.—*New Orleans Bee.*
Bubbling over with brightness and life.—*News and Courier.*
Cooper De Leon's brilliant Christmas story.—*Courier-Journal.*
A delicious brochure of fun and sentiment.—*Washington Gazette.*
A pleasant, breezy, altogether lovable story.—*Nashville American.*

*MAILED, PREPAID, ON RECEIPT OF 50 CENTS, BY*

L. Bindery.

### THE GOSSIP PRINTING CO.,
#### MOBILE, ALA.